Also by Chris Priestley

The Dead of Winter
Mister Creecher
Through Dead Eyes

***

The Tales of Terror Collection:
Uncle Montague's Tales of Terror
Tales of Terror from the Black Ship
Tales of Terror from the Tunnel's Mouth
Christmas Tales of Terror

THE DEAD MEN STOOD TOGETHER

CHRIS PRIESTLEY

BLOOMSBURY

LONDON NEW DELHI NEW YORK SYDNEY

Bloomsbury Publishing, London, New Delhi, New York and Sydney

First published in Great Britain in September 2013
by Bloomsbury Publishing Plc
50 Bedford Square, London WC1B 3DP

www.bloomsbury.com

Bloomsbury is a registered trademark of Bloomsbury Publishing Plc

This paperback edition published in October 2014

Copyright © Chris Priestley 2013

The moral rights of the author have been asserted

The extracts from *The Rime of the Ancient Mariner* by
Samuel Taylor Coleridge are taken from the 1858 edition,
published by Sampson Low, Son & Co, London.

A CIP catalogue record for this book is available from the British Library

ISBN 978 1 4088 4302 4

Typeset by Hewer Text UK Ltd, Edinburgh
Printed and bound in Great Britain by CPI Group (UK) Ltd, Croydon CR0 4YY

1 3 5 7 9 10 8 6 4 2

For Isabel

I pass, like night, from land to land;
I have strange power of speech;
That moment that his face I see,
I know the man that must hear me:
To him my tale I teach.

The old man shuffles to a halt and stands for a moment, head bowed, shaking a little, holding on to his staff. He looks at the end of his days – but then he's looked that way for a long, long time.

Is he more exhausted by the walk he's just made across the moors, or by the thought of the miles he will walk tomorrow? Maybe it's just the weight of all those years of guilt. I don't much care.

He's suffered long and hard, but so have I. I'll waste no sympathy on him. His death would free us both, but, spiteful to the last, he seems to go on and on. Maybe he's immortal, for we've walked together for centuries now. Soon it will be nineteen hundred years since the birth of Jesus.

Our dress is very different from those about us, but there is something in the magic that surrounds us that means I'm hardly noticed at all. I'm seen and yet not seen. I flit like a thought into the heads of those I pass, and then that thought flies on and I am forgotten in an instant.

The old man's clothes are no more than shabby rags and his long hair and beard, both frosted white, mark him as a travelling beggar and nothing more. There are plenty enough of them in this new age, just as there were of old.

We're back in our own country. We're once again in England after so many years in foreign parts. It's different now, and yet the same, like the ghost of the girl still visible in an old woman's face.

The old fellow sits down on a low wall and leans the tall staff against it, resting his bony arms on his wasted thighs. I can see his lips moving silently. Is he praying? Are you praying, you old sinner?

It's cold. The leaves have fallen from the trees and redwings hunt among the tangled hedge for the last of the berries. The old man shivers and hunches his shoulders.

He pretends he doesn't know I'm here, but we both know he does. I'm always here. We're tied together and he knows it. We might each of us wish it weren't so, but it is and there's not a thing either of us can do about it.

He lifts his head. He raises his eyes and looks at me. As soon as he sees me, I watch the usual burst of pain rack his body. After a moment, he looks at me again, his face pale and contorted, his eyes sunken. He searches my face for something – pity? – but finds nothing of comfort. He closes his eyes and hangs his head.

A young man walks past me, dressed in black, a scarf tied round his neck. He pays me no heed. He seems caught up in his own thoughts, muttering quietly to himself.

He's a big man, with black unruly hair. His clothes, though respectable, are also a little shabby. He seems absent-minded. His large eyes are watery and he has the air of a sleepwalker about him.

All in all, he has the look of someone cultured but not someone of any means. Perhaps he is a country parson or schoolteacher. Whoever he is, his life is about to change for ever.

Bells ring out from the church tower in the town. A horse and cart rumbles by and the man stands aside and finds himself beside the old tramp, who he had clearly not noticed till then. He looks at him with his large, kind eyes.

The young man is about to speak – perhaps to ask if he can be of any help – when the old man's hand shoots out like a snake and clutches at the stranger's sleeve. He tries to pull away, telling the old man to leave him be. He does so with good humour. But there is a quiver of fear in his voice. As well there might be.

The young man tells him that he is expected somewhere – that friends are waiting for him – that he has to go. I almost feel sorry for him. He has no idea what he is about to hear. He asks again, his voice more pleading now, for the old man to leave hold.

But he doesn't let go.

'There was a ship,' begins the old man hoarsely.

The young man laughs but his patience begins to fade and again he tells the old man to leave him be. His tone is angry now and the old man looses his grip. But it means nothing. His true hold on the young man is only just beginning. He fixes him with his shadowed eyes, twinkling like rock pools. The young man becomes still.

Though I have watched this scene acted out a thousand times before, it still pulls me in: the moment when the old man traps his prey. The young man sits alongside the wizened old traveller, staring intently at his leathery face. Passers-by who had noticed the old man stop the stranger, now seem not to see either of them at all and continue on their way without giving a sideways glance.

And so the old man begins his tale: a tale I have heard many, many times before. In any event, I hardly need to hear it told. It's not something I'm ever likely to forget. I was there, after all, though you would scarcely know it by the way he tells the story.

You'd think you might have more than a passing word to say about your own nephew, you old liar! Yes, that's right: that withered old bag of bones over there is my uncle. My own flesh and blood, heaven help me.

He is my own father's brother. He hails from the same West Country town that I do, though so much time has gone by now I no longer feel that we were kin at all. I wish we weren't.

It is a sure sign of a lack of any knowledge of the world when country folk tell you that their own particular patch of land is the best in all the world, but that is exactly what I once thought of my small stretch of the Somerset coast.

And strange to say that though I have travelled far and wide, I still feel the same. All those years I spent dreaming of foreign lands and now I have the same yearning for my home.

I would give anything to see my home again, though I know that everyone and everything I knew will long since have turned to dust.

Even so, I would love, just one more time, to walk the moss-floored oak woods, to stand on the harbour wall or skim pebbles across the breakers as I once did. These things are like a dream to me now. They are like words written in mist.

And yet they are there still in my memory and perhaps I can make them live again. But where to start my story? Which beginning shall I choose? Yes, I think it must start on the day I saw the pilot's son in the woods . . .

PART THE FIRST

I

We lived in a little hunchbacked cottage on a tree-lined track that led out from the town and up into the wooded slopes beyond. We went to the town regularly to sell our wares – my mother made baskets – and to buy provisions, but we saw few people at the cottage.

It was a small place but comfortable and, like many others of those times, with a wooden frame and thatched roof across the house and the adjoining barn. Dog roses climbed over the garden fence and honeysuckle grew over the porch.

My mother had a little vegetable patch where she grew beans and cabbages, and a small orchard of apple and plum trees, and beyond that lay the woods of oak and hazel that coated the slopes leading down to the pebble beaches below.

I slept in the top of the house, the beams crowding in around me. My father had cut me a round window in the gable end and I could crouch on my bed and look out across our vegetable patch and towards the woods. I loved to look at the woods at night and hear the owls and, sometimes, in warmer weather, the nightingales that lived there.

My parents had taught me all about the nature of the local fields – my father about the animals and birds, my mother about the plants and flowers and trees. I could name almost anything we came across by the time I was seven.

Often, if I couldn't sleep and the weather wasn't too cold, I would take down the round shutter my father had made to cover the window at night and I'd look out at the night woods and wonder what animals went about their unseen business among the trees.

One summer evening as shadows grew, I was kneeling on my bed and looking out when I saw a figure I knew well, standing in the clearing beyond my mother's little vegetable patch. My mother was dozing in her chair by the open back door and scarcely noticed me passing as I went out.

The pilot's son stood exactly where I had seen him from the window. He hadn't moved a muscle. I walked slowly towards him, stealthily, not wishing to frighten him.

The pilot, who steered a safe course through the treacherous shallows for ships coming in and out of the bay, had been a good friend of my father. They'd known each other since they were children. He'd been kind to us since my father died. I had a strong suspicion that he bought more baskets from my mother than he could ever use.

And I had known the pilot's son all my childhood, but I could not say we were friends exactly as he had always been something of a strange boy. We had played together as young children, but as he got older, more and more, he entered into a world of his own making and we didn't talk as true friends might.

He was pale-skinned with pitch-black hair and eyes that seemed a size too large for his thin and delicate features. He was always out and about, come rain or shine, but his smooth, wan skin was like that of a newborn infant.

His hands were long and thin fingered and those fingers seemed as though they were without bones. When he made gestures – as he often did, for no obvious reason – they moved like seaweed fronds in the tide.

'Hello!' I whispered, following his gaze.

He didn't respond and I was about to speak again when he turned to face me. He appeared to take a moment to remember who I was. Then his eyes opened wide.

'The Devil is coming to your house,' he said, all of a sudden.

I was momentarily startled, as you can perhaps imagine. But then little of what the pilot's boy said made any sense. It was better not to try to make sense of it. On this occasion, for some reason, I decided to humour him.

'What do you mean?' I said with a nervous chuckle.

He looked at me with an odd expression, a little surprised, no doubt, that I was actually trying to understand him. He searched my face for any sign that I was joking at his expense.

'The Devil,' he repeated, as though I had been too stupid to understand his meaning the first time.

'What are you talking about?'

'I saw him,' he said, pointing to his head. 'In here.'

'And did he have horns and goat's feet? Was he lit by flames?'

The pilot's boy regarded me for a moment and then shook his head, as though it was not worth the effort to explain to me. Then, seeming to change his mind, he turned back and spoke again.

'I don't know about the things you say,' he said. 'But he is the Devil.'

He looked so serious; I had to find out more.

'And he was going to my house? You're sure?'

The pilot's son nodded solemnly but said nothing more. I shrugged, uncertain whether to continue this conversation or just let him grow bored with it. Somehow I couldn't let it go.

'He was probably just a customer wanting to order some baskets from my mother,' I said. 'What did he look like? Maybe I know him.'

The pilot's son frowned and cocked his head, closing his eyes clearly trying to picture the scene.

'He had a rabbit in one hand, two birds in the other,' he continued.

I shrugged and raised my eyebrows.

'What?' I said, confused.

The pilot's son opened his eyes. The huge pupils shrank until they were pinpricks.

'He carried a rabbit in one hand. In the other two birds.'

'How was he dressed?' I asked, more and more confused.

'Like a man,' said the pilot's boy. 'But he wears a cross on his chest and has another on his back that mocks the first – for it kills as the other saves.'

I was baffled. The image of this man – if man he was – was getting stranger and stranger, but I felt I had to try to make sense of it.

'I'm sure you're mistaken,' I said. 'I'm sure he was just a man like any other.'

The pilot's boy frowned at me. He shook his head.

'But why then did he have so many demons with him?' he said.

'Demons?' I asked in amazement. 'What do you mean?'

The pilot's boy looked down and shook his head rapidly, and clenched and flexed his long fingers. I had seen this before. Whenever he reached a point where he did not want to explain any more, he closed his eyes and shook his head, and – as he did now – ran away, flapping his arms like a bird and squawking.

II

Though I knew the words of the pilot's boy to be nonsense, they bothered me. I was still thinking about what he'd said when a hand touched me on the shoulder and I almost jumped into the branches of a nearby tree.

'What has my young friend been telling you?'

I turned, relieved to see a smiling, bearded face I knew well. It was the hermit who lived alone in the oak woods that covered the hills thereabouts. He lived in a hut among the trees on a hillside by the sea. It was nothing more than a pile of sticks held together by honeysuckle and moss. How he survived there in winter, no one knew.

I liked him and would often seek him out when I had no work to do. He would give me some nettle tea and tell me stories. They were strange stories, and though I did not always know exactly what he meant by them, I liked his voice and I liked the way my brain seemed to quiver after listening to them, as if he had roused some part of it that had been sleeping and it woke, confused and restless.

'I don't know,' I said finally, in answer to his question. 'He talks so oddly. Why is he like that?'

The hermit laced his fingers together.

'Some say he is a changeling,' he said matter-of-factly. 'That the elfin folk took the pilot's baby and swapped him for one of their own.'

I stared off in the direction in which the boy had gone.

'Do you believe that?' I asked.

The hermit shrugged.

'Perhaps,' he said. 'He has the look of an elfin child about him.'

It was true. There was something other-worldly about his appearance.

'I just thought he was crazy,' I said.

'Crazy?' said the hermit, waving his hand in front of his face dismissively. 'That word can cover many things, my boy. Perhaps he sees things that we cannot.'

'But how do you know he sees anything?' I asked.

The hermit shrugged again.

'How would I know that he does not?'

I smiled.

'I knew a man who went mad,' said the hermit as he set off walking back to his home among the trees with me following behind. 'He thought to himself that we are not really, truly, here at all.'

'Not here?' I said.

'Not truly,' continued the hermit. 'His thought was that we were all players in another man's dream.'

I frowned. The hermit continued.

'At first it was an idle thought,' he said. 'We have all had such fancies, after all.'

I had never had such a fancy, but I kept it to myself for fear the hermit would think me dull. We reached the hermit's nest of branches and twigs. A fire burned nearby and we sat down on a log beside it.

'But gradually,' said the hermit, 'this thought took root, like ivy in a wall. It wormed itself through the mortar and slowly dislodged brick after brick until his mind came tumbling down.'

'And what happened to him?' I asked.

'He threw himself from the church tower of the town in which he lived,' he said. 'He was sure that he could come to no harm because in truth he was only a phantasm in another man's sleeping mind.'

'He was wrong then,' I said. 'For I'm just as sure he dashed his brains out when he hit the ground.'

The hermit nodded.

'He did,' he said. 'Most certainly, he did. But that doesn't disprove his theory.'

'How?' I said.

'Because perhaps the sleeping man dreamt a dream in which a man thought himself to be in a dream and in that dream he threw himself from a church tower and killed himself.'

I frowned, trying to take in what the hermit said. He laughed. But I was troubled by this line of thought and was not so easily diverted from it.

'Perhaps we make the world ourselves,' he said. 'Perhaps we invent it all at every moment. Perhaps all things are dead until we give them life with our imaginations. Perhaps there are a million worlds, each one existing only for that one person and none other.'

I shook my head dizzily.

'I don't understand,' I said.

The hermit smiled.

'I shouldn't boggle your brain with such notions,' he said.

'I don't mind,' I said. 'I like having my brain boggled.'

I picked up a twig that lay at my feet and held it to my face. It was encrusted with several sorts of lichen, yellow, white and pale grey. Some covered the bark whilst others formed a kind of forest of branches that echoed in miniature the wood we sat in. Worlds within worlds.

It was late now. Night was coming in and draining all the colours from the scene. The hermit's fire glowed more intensely and threw our shadows on the trees and on the mossy woodland floor. What colour is moss at twilight? Not green, nor any colour known by name.

A nightingale began to sing in the trees nearby, its voice startling us both and then holding us in its grip for the length of its song.

'Some say it is a sad song,' whispered the hermit, as reverently as if we had been in church and the bird's song had been a sermon. 'But I don't think of it that way.'

The bird let loose another burst of its song. And I had to agree that it didn't make me feel sad at all. It lifted my heart and made the whole wood come alive, as though it had been waiting for the nightingale to sing.

'The pilot's boy says that he sees spirits,' said the hermit. 'He says that in the air around us are different spirits, good and bad. They are attracted to us depending on our characters. A wholly good person will attract only good spirits.'

I thought of the man the pilot's son said he had seen, and the demons he brought with him.

'And a bad person?'

'A bad person will attract bad spirits – demons, the boy calls them,' said the hermit. 'And that must mean that there are many more demons in the air than angels.'

'Is that why you live out here on your own,' I asked, 'because you think people are bad?'

The hermit looked at me very seriously.

'No,' he said, shaking his head. 'I don't shun people because I am better than they are. I shun them because I do not deserve to be with other people. I shun them as a penance.'

He looked away, deep in thought.

'You don't *really* believe he sees these spirits?' I asked.

'I do believe he sees them,' said the hermit. 'Whether they are there or not, I couldn't say. And whether they have the meaning he gives them, I likewise couldn't guarantee.'

'Surely demons could only be bad,' I said with a grin.

To my surprise, the hermit did not agree.

'Perhaps. But perhaps we need demons to drive us to good things,' he said. 'Perhaps they are neither good nor bad, but simply some vital part of the world, like air or water.'

I frowned.

'Come,' said the hermit. 'It's getting dark. Time you were home.'

'I'm fine,' I said, getting up. 'There's no need to go with me.'

'Nonsense,' he said with a smile. 'With the air full of demons, I would feel happier making sure that you got safely to your house. Your mother would expect it of me.'

I smiled. The hermit walked with me until I could see my cottage and then I realised that he was no longer there and I turned to see him standing alone in the moon shadows. I waved and he waved back, then he walked away.

III

My home was dark against the western sky and bats flitted here and there as I approached, picking off the moths lured to the lamplight shining from the window.

I was walking towards the house when I noticed another light coming from the barn and, looking through the door, saw a man standing with his back to me, splashing water from a bucket into his face as he leaned forward. A lamp was resting on a barrel.

I stood there staring. He pulled his shirt over his head and his back was now bared. Written all across it in ink scratched into the flesh were all manner of signs and symbols – stars and moons and curious devices I did not know or understand.

'Who are you, sir?' I asked, as strongly as I was able. He turned at my voice.

He was a tall man, thin but with his muscles well defined. His face was long and handsome in a wolfish way. His beard was short and darker than his hair, which was wet and fell to his shoulders. His smile was wide and white.

'Well, then,' he said. 'And who might this be?'

I said nothing. I was staring at his chest, which was likewise inscribed with pictures. There was the sun and the moon, a ship in full sail. There were coiling snakes and knotted ropes. There was a cloud with a lightning bolt, dice, a death's head.

'The pictures bother you, boy?' he said. 'Here, let's hide them away.'

He grabbed his shirt and pulled it on over his head. At that point my mother appeared and I moved towards her stealthily; whether to protect her or be protected by her, I could not rightly say. The stranger laughed – and to my surprise, my mother joined him.

'Do you not know me then?' said the stranger.

I looked to my mother in confusion. She chuckled and shook her head.

''Tis your uncle,' she said. 'Your father's brother. He played with you many times when you were a little boy.'

I did remember my uncle. Or at least I loved the memory of him and his laugh and his wonderful stories. But I couldn't match that memory to the man who stood before me. My uncle seemed to read my mind.

'I have changed a little,' he said. 'I have been through many trials since we last met. But then we all have changed over the past years, have we not? Apart from my sister-in-law there, who looks younger, and more beautiful if anything.'

My mother blushed – something I hadn't seen her do since my father was alive. She slapped him with the back of her hand and he pretended that he was hurt and staggered back, groaning and clutching his stomach.

I laughed and he looked up smiling and opened his arms. After a moment's hesitation, I strode forward and we embraced. I was suddenly overcome with memories of my father and had to fight to hold back tears. Again he seemed to sense what I was thinking.

'I was right sorry to hear about your father,' he said. 'He was a good man, my brother. And they are rarer than rubies, let me tell you.'

My mother said my uncle must eat and we all went through into the kitchen, where the whole room was filled with delicious smells. I walked to the pot and took the lid off.

'Rabbit?' I said.

'Your uncle brought it,' said my mother. 'And two pigeons.'

I thought of the pilot's boy and realised now that my uncle was the stranger he had seen.

'They were in my path,' he said with a shrug. 'It seemed wrong to come empty-handed.'

'How . . .' I said. 'How did you –'

'I have a crossbow,' said my uncle.

I saw too that he wore a cross around his neck. *'Another on his back that mocks the first.'* No doubt my uncle wore his crossbow on his back.

'You must be a good shot,' I said.

'Well now,' he said, taking a piece of bread, 'there's not a lot of use in having one if you're not, is there?'

'I don't know . . .' I said.

The cross around my uncle's neck was a large wooden crucifix. He saw me looking at it and grinned.

'A wise old monk gave me this,' he said. 'In thanks for saving him from a heathen who was about to inflict some of the pains of the saints upon him.'

'Really?' I said, wide-eyed.

'Aye,' he said. ''Twas in the Mountains of the Moon in the Arab lands. We had marched five days in burning heat in search of a treasure we had been told about in the port we had been besieging. But there was no treasure.'

He shook his head.

'I have been so close so many times, but the treasure is always somewhere else, in someone else's hands. One day, it will be different.'

'Treasure?' I asked.

'Aye!' he said. 'It's out there, lad. More treasure than you've ever dreamt of.'

My uncle grinned and leaned across to tousle my hair. My mother carried the pot to the table and ladled some of the stew into my uncle's bowl.

'Is no one joining me?' he asked.

'We've already eaten,' said my mother, but, seeing my pleading face, she fetched another bowl and put it in front of me.

'That's better,' said my uncle. 'We need to feed you up, lad. Look at you. Skin and bone.'

'He's only a boy,' said my mother. 'Leave him be.'

We tucked into our rabbit stew and a contented silence reigned for a few minutes.

'Are you a soldier, then?' I asked.

He smiled a strange smile and fingered the cross around his neck.

'I have been many things, lad,' he said. 'Not all of which I'm proud of. I'm a mariner first and foremost. But I've had my fill of fighting other men's battles.'

'Good,' said my mother. 'There is always a home for you here.'

'Here?' said my uncle. 'No. I love you dearly but I cannot stay here. I'm not made for this life. I never was.'

My mother looked away, as though remembering old arguments.

'No,' continued my uncle. 'I am going to seek my fortune. There are riches to be had in the East Indies and why should it not be me who grabs them?'

He saw my eyes widen. Not at the mention of riches, but at the mention of the East Indies – and my mother saw it too.

'You are sailing to the Pacific?' I asked excitedly.

'Aye,' he said. 'That I am. The Spice Islands. Japan.'

'You've been before?'

'Aye. I've sailed to the East Indies and Japan. China too. I've stood inside the pleasure dome at Xanadu that Kubla Khan had built at his decree. There are wonders in the East – wonders no opium eater could ever hope to dream of.'

My eyes were so wide I feared they might pop out of my head.

'But that means sailing round Cape Horn,' I said. 'They say it's the most dangerous voyage there is.'

He smiled.

'Aye,' he said, as though danger was a fine wine to be savoured. 'They do. And with some good cause.'

He smiled and leaned back in his chair, clasping his hands behind his head.

'I sail with a group of adventurers,' he said. 'They are rich – which is necessary for such an enterprise – but they are also peacocks who are more at home with their jewellers or tailors than they are slitting a man's throat.'

'You've slit a man's throat, Uncle?' I asked, startled.

'When it has been necessary to do so.'

'I'd rather not hear this kind of talk,' said my mother with a frown.

'You're right,' my uncle said. 'It's not anything to talk lightly of. Every man's death is a sacred thing.'

'Surely it is life that is sacred,' said my mother.

My uncle shrugged.

'The same thing in the end.'

My mother sighed but said no more.

'Maybe you'd like me to teach you how to fire a crossbow, lad,' said my uncle.

'Yes!' I said excitedly.

'You'll do no such thing if I –' began my mother.

'Peace. No arguments.' My uncle held up his hands. 'I'm not here long. We sail in a few days.'

'So soon?' said my mother.

'I'm sorry.' He reached out and touched her arm with his long fingers. 'But I shall be rich one day, I promise you, and then I shall send for you both and –'

'I shan't leave,' said my mother. 'My mother, father and husband are all in the churchyard and I'll join them one day.'

My uncle laughed.

'Look at you!' he said. 'How old are you now? You can't be more than twenty-five years old.'

'I'm thirty-eight, as you well know.'

'There's time enough to talk of dying, all the same,' he replied.

'This is my home,' said my mother. 'I've never wanted more.'

My uncle smiled.

'I know you haven't,' he said and he winked at me. My mother saw it and scowled.

My uncle leaned over and gave her a kiss.

'Peace,' he said again. 'I'm teasing you. Some

are made to wander and some not. There's no right or wrong. We're all made different.'

My mother smiled, but I knew that smile – it was a keeping-the-peace smile. It said, 'I have more to say, but I'm choosing not to.' I knew it well and I had the impression that my uncle had seen it a few times himself.

He proved himself to be a man who is happy with the sound of his own voice, and we were happy listeners, as he told of his adventures in exotic places we had scarcely heard of.

We'd not quite heard the story of each scar he chose to show us, when my mother said that she must away to bed and that I must do the same, for we had a buyer coming by close after dawn to collect some crabbing pots.

My uncle declared he was tired too, but refused my offer to give him my bed, saying that he wasn't sure he could sleep in a bed after years of sleeping on rocks and in ditches and the holds of rat-infested ships. He swore that our barn would be luxury in comparison. And with more embraces and a noisy yawn, he said his goodnights and retreated to the barn.

I went to my room and looked out of my window, out past the roof of the barn in which my uncle made his rest and towards the woods and the hermit. All the warm glow that had built up in our kitchen seemed to drift out through that round window and be replaced by a sudden chill.

The words of the pilot's boy came back to me and, though I should not have let his foolish talk upset me, it did. I spent a restless night, my dreams troubled by those pictures scrawled into my uncle's skin and by the thought of the air alive with demons.

IV

I woke very early, before anyone else stirred, and lay in my bed in a waking dream and ahead of me, in my dreaming, was the open ocean. I had always felt in my heart that this was where my future lay. The menfolk of our family had all been mariners for as long as anyone could recall.

And I don't mean fisherfolk. Don't get me wrong – I've nothing against fishermen. They are brave enough and do a job that's needed. But I'm talking about true mariners here.

My family had sailed the seven seas. They'd served in the navy and fought for their country. They'd crewed merchant ships trading with distant empires. They'd seen things most men only dream of – and more than a few things that most men would be glad to dismiss as a nightmare and nothing more.

My own father was a mariner and, like so many of that kind before him, had lost his life to the sea, swallowed up by it in a storm that likewise took the lives of most of his crew. I knew many of them and had known them since I was a little boy and my mother had taken me down to the harbour. I would be there to see my father sail out and cheer him as he came home.

I couldn't wait to get a chance to climb aboard my father's ship and would have sailed away with him when I was five, had he or my mother let me. I sailed with him often on shorter voyages and learned many of the skills and crafts of sailing men. I should have sailed with him on his last and fatal voyage, but I was ill and could not go.

Another ship saw my father's go under and, though they tried to come to their aid, the seas were too high and they managed to pick up only a handful of men, and my father was not among them. I was twelve years old when we heard of his death.

The news hit my mother like a bolt of lightning. She cried and cried until I feared she would never stop, and in looking after her and looking after the business when she was too beaten down to work, I could hide the fact that I did not feel the same pain.

I did feel pain, but it was a bitter pain – it was the pain of feeling I had never really known my father and that now I never could. It was the pain of not feeling the pain I knew I should.

I wished I could have loved him as the mourners at his funeral had loved him, but I had never seen what they had seen. He'd never shown that to me. He had taught me all I knew about the sea, but the man himself was a mystery to me.

My mother was sure it was providence that I had been spared my father's fate and refused to let me sail again. She had her own business as a basket maker, selling baskets and crabbing pots to the fisherfolk, and she made me learn the skills of their making and help her in the selling.

Inside, I felt that this was no work for a man – and certainly not a sailing man – but I couldn't bear to give my mother any further sadness, so I kept my complaints to myself and helped her as best I could. In time, I came to enjoy my days with her and miss the sea as something I'd known once but would not know again.

Now my uncle was here, home from wandering and ready for more, and I was once again filled with a terrible yearning to see the world.

V

When the sun's rays began to light my room, I got dressed, crept past my mother's room and went stealthily into the barn, where my uncle still slept. He looked like a dead man. He barely made a sound with his breathing and he made no movement at all. He lay on his back, hands clasped together across his chest.

He was fully dressed, the purse and dagger still round his waist. The crossbow was leaning up against a wooden post. My mother would never let him teach me to fire it, I knew it. I looked at my uncle and then reached for the crossbow.

As soon as my hands touched it, I felt myself dragged sideways and something sharp pressed against my neck. Looking up, I saw my uncle leaning over me, his dagger pointed at my windpipe. He shook his head and let me go.

I scrabbled backwards through the dirt until I

reached the wall and then sat staring at him. He was putting his dagger back in his scabbard.

'You'll get yourself killed, creeping up on a man like that,' he said.

'Sorry,' was all I could think to say.

He turned and smiled.

'No – it's me who should be sorry,' he said. 'I've lived my life among thieves and scoundrels. I'm not fit for decent people.'

My heart was still leaping about like a rabbit in a sack.

'You really do have a look of your father about you,' said my uncle, stretching and rubbing the sleep from his eyes.

'Did you know him well?' I asked.

'Know him?' He said with a laugh. 'Of course I knew him. he was my brother! He was a good man. He was a tough man too, despite his gentle ways. I liked him. He never had too much time for me though.'

'Why?' I asked, calming a little.

'We were different animals,' said my uncle. 'He thought I was reckless and a dreamer. And he was right. We can't help how we're made. I always wanted to know what was over the horizon. He was a fine sailor, your father, but I could never understand why he never wanted to sail on and explore. But then he had you and your mother to come home to.'

My uncle's smile faded and he looked away.

'Were you never married, Uncle?' I asked.

'Me?' he said. 'No. Well, almost – once. A long time ago. But I'd have made a poor husband and an even poorer father.'

He turned to me and peered at me intently.

'And what about you? Do you dream of distant shores?'

'I used to,' I said, lowering my voice a little in case my mother walked by. 'But I don't sail any more. I help my mother now. Ever since my father died . . .'

My uncle nodded.

'She's lucky to have a good son.'

'She wants me safe,' I said.

'Safe?' said my uncle, as though he had never used the word in his entire life. 'And is that what you want? To be safe?'

'I have porridge ready on the stove,' said a voice behind him. It was my mother, standing in the doorway. I jumped to my feet. I saw the look in her eyes and knew she had been listening. She grabbed hold of my uncle's arm as I walked out of the barn and headed towards the house.

'I told you – leave him be,' she said.

'What sort of life is this for a boy with the sea in his veins?' said my uncle.

'It's none of your concern,' said my mother quietly, but with more anger than I think I'd ever heard in her voice.

We ate our porridge in silence and my mother ate very little at all. When he'd finished his bowl, my uncle said that he would sleep aboard the ship that night.

'There's no need for that,' said my mother with a sigh.

'I wouldn't want to stay where I'm not wanted,' he said, winking at me.

My mother saw him and slapped his arm with the back of her hand.

'I'll not be here long,' said my uncle. 'Once you have a crew it's best to get them to sea before they start to wander. Leave them ashore for a couple of days and half of them will be married or in the town jail.'

'When will you be back?' asked my mother.

My uncle shrugged and stood up.

'Who can say?' he said with a grin. 'Maybe some far-off tribe will make me a king.'

Mother smiled and shook her head.

'You'll never change, will you?'

'No,' said my uncle. 'Probably not.'

He leaned forward, resting his hands on the table.

'I promise you,' he went on with great serious-ness, 'when I make my fortune, I'll come back here and you shall want for nothing. You shall never do another day's work and you shall be the finest lady in this town.'

My mother laughed.

'You promised me that when you were ten and I was eight,' she said. 'Do you remember?'

'Aye,' he said. 'I remember. I meant it then and I mean it now. But you chose my brother.'

My mother blushed and opened her mouth to speak.

'You made the right choice,' said my uncle. 'He was a better man than me. We both knew it.'

They stood looking at each other for a moment in silence, seeming to have forgotten all about me until my uncle turned and smiled.

'I'm sorry if I frightened you back there,' he said.

My mother cast me a worried glance.

'No,' I said, trying my best to sound as though I had a dagger put to my throat every week. 'I wasn't frightened.'

My uncle laughed, seeing my bravado for what it was. But it wasn't an unkind laugh.

'That's the spirit,' he said, playfully punching me in the chest.

VI

I spent the day with my mother and I'm sorry to say I was not good company, making it very plain that I would rather have been elsewhere. But she either did not notice or did not rise to the bait. My mother was so good-hearted she could easily ride such a timid storm.

The shadows were long by the time my uncle returned. He walked up the lane singing a song to himself. It was in a foreign tongue and had a mournful sound to it.

'Hello!' he said, hailing me with a broad grin. 'And how are you, my friend?'

'I'm well, Uncle,' I said.

He put his arm round my shoulder and we walked together towards the cottage.

'You look like a man with something on his mind,' said my uncle. 'If you don't mind me saying.'

It was true.

'You promised that you would teach me how to shoot your crossbow.'

He rested his hand on my shoulder and smiled.

'I did not promise,' he said. 'I'd be happy to, but we must ask your mother what she thinks about it.'

I twisted my face and groaned.

'I'm sorry,' he said. 'But that's how it must be. I have given your mother enough cause to be angry with me over the years and I'd like us to part on good terms when I sail.'

I saw that there was no point in resisting. I saw too that my mother would never allow such a thing. My uncle read all this in my face and smiled a cock-eyed grin.

'I'll have a word with your mother,' he said. 'She's not as obstinate as she seems.'

I nodded and let him go ahead of me into the cottage. After a few moments, I could hear the sound of voices from within, and soon after that the angry tone of my mother.

My uncle's voice was calm and even through-out and, after a short while, my mother's voice calmed too, and to my great surprise my uncle emerged with a triumphant smile on his face.

'But know that if he gets hurt,' shouted my mother from inside, 'I will take that crossbow and –'

I never did get to hear what my mother was going to do with the crossbow, because my uncle hustled me away towards the barn, where we fetched the actual weapon and set off towards the orchard.

'Do you really think my father was a good man?' I asked.

'Aye,' said my uncle. 'Why would I say it if it wasn't true?'

'To keep my mother sweet?' I ventured.

He stopped and smiled at me.

'That is possible,' he said. 'But in this case it was my true opinion. Besides, do you not know it to be true yourself?'

I took a deep breath, wary of being too forthcoming with a man I barely knew.

'I can remember little about him,' I said. 'He was always leaving to go to sea.'

'But he loved you dearly,' said my uncle.

'He didn't show it,' I returned.

'Some men don't. Some men can't.'

'Then maybe some men shouldn't be fathers,' I said, my voice cracking, my face reddening. 'Nor husbands neither.'

My uncle turned away and looked into the woods.

'If you want to learn to fire a crossbow,' he said, 'then I'm your man. If you want someone to wipe your nose and hold your hand, then you must look elsewhere.'

I was struck by the coldness of his words and they shocked me out of my impending tears.

'I'm no wet nurse, boy,' he said, as though there had ever been a doubt. 'It's not in my nature.'

After a moment, he handed the crossbow to me. 'Shall we fire some bolts?'

I nodded and took the weapon from him. I was surprised by its weight. It was made of wood and metal and it had patterns carved into both.

'Hold it so it's pointing to the ground.'

I did as he said, and put my foot through a hoop he called the stirrup – and it did look just like the stirrup on a horse's saddle – and turned a handle until the string was pulled back taut and held in place by a catch, the bow bending and creaking as I did so.

This was the great thing about the crossbow, explained my uncle – that a mere boy like me could operate it. No strength was required, as with a longbow, although skill was still required in the shooting.

'One day,' he said, 'all battles will be between men armed with machines like this.'

I tried to imagine such a thing as I leaned the

crossbow on a fence rail and lifted the stock to my shoulder. I reached under it to grasp the firing mechanism – a long twisted metal lever. My uncle placed a bolt in front of the string.

'Don't jerk it,' he said. 'Choose your target. Squeeze when you're ready to fire.'

Just as I focused on the sapling I was to shoot at, a bird landed on a branch and cheeped, distracting me, and I turned the crossbow towards it and then the bird leapt up in a burst of feathers and fell to the ground.

I had shot it. I hadn't meant to. I can't say how or why my finger pulled the lever, but pull it it did. Carrying the crossbow with me, I walked over to where the bird was lying, impaled on the bolt which ran through its neck.

It was a nightingale. It still twitched pitifully and without a moment's thought my uncle stood on its throat and finished it off.

'If that was meant, that was quite a shot!' he said, patting me on the back.

I pulled away angrily.

'Meant?' I said. 'I didn't mean to do it. It was an accident.'

My uncle smiled.

'Very well,' he said. 'No harm done. 'Tis only a bird, after all.'

But I stared down at that bird with a heavy heart. I had done a terrible thing and I knew it, even if my uncle did not.

'I feel bad about it. I wish I hadn't done it.'

My uncle put his hand on my shoulder.

'Guilt?' he said. 'It's a waste of energy, my friend.'

'I can't help feeling guilty,' I replied.

'You'd be surprised,' said my uncle. 'I have done many things I should feel guilty about but do not. I stopped feeling guilty a long time ago. There is no point to it.'

I frowned and shrugged. I didn't know what to say.

'Will the bird come back to life?' he asked. 'Will it change anything?'

'Well, no –'

'And you say it was an accident anyway?'

'Yes, but –'

'Well, then,' he said, clapping his hands and grinning. 'There is nothing to feel guilty about.'

He shepherded me towards the house.

'Is all well?' said my mother as we approached.

'Aye,' said my uncle. 'He's only upset because he couldn't hit the target. But I told him it was only his first time and he shouldn't be hard on himself.

'Your uncle's right,' said my mother. 'You can't

expect to master something in the first few moments.'

I was grateful to my uncle at the time for saying nothing of the bird. My mother would have been as upset as I was by its wanton killing. But I later suspected that the lie was for his own benefit, not mine, for he knew my mother would have blamed him and not me.

That night, when I looked from my window out towards where my uncle had left the bird, having taken the bolt from its body, I saw the pilot's son.

He lifted up the bird in his hands and looked at the house, mouthing words I could not hear. I ducked down, fearing he would see me. When I eventually felt it safe to look, he was gone.

I closed the shutter and lay back on my bed. I slept and dreamt: dreamt of battles and the fizz of crossbow bolts.

I dreamt too of that sad and lifeless nightingale.

VII

The following day my uncle, as he took his leave of us, told us the ship was ready and he would return later in the day for one last farewell.

My mother cried. I stood beside her and watched as he walked away down the lane heading towards the harbour. It felt like my last chance of escape was sailing away.

My mother sensed this, I think, though she said nothing. I could feel it somehow through the skin of the hand she placed gently against my face before she turned and walked back to the house.

I stayed where I was, looking down the now deserted lane, catching the faint whiff of seaweed and the cry of seagulls on the breeze.

But as soon as he was gone, thoughts of the nightingale faded and were replaced by dreams of sailing, of exploring, of adventuring. All that day, I could think of nothing else but my uncle and his intended voyage. My mind quivered with images of Japan and the islands of the East. Where these images came from, I couldn't say, for I had no idea of what those places looked like.

Every chore I did seemed more dull, every pail of water heavier than it had ever been before. The minutes seemed to last for hours, the hours for an eternity.

When my uncle did at last return to the cottage, he told us that his ship was set to leave before the dawn, sailing on the next tide.

We ate our last meal together and, though my uncle once again entertained us with tales of his adventures and treasure-hunting, it was a melancholy affair. We embraced and tears were shed.

And though I was exhausted when night fell, I couldn't sleep. I turned this way and that, and every time I closed my eyes I imagined I was in the hold of some ship bound for foreign lands.

The wind blew round the eaves of the house and it sounded like sailcloth filling, and every other noise recalled the creak of timbers or the lapping of the waves against the hull.

I had put the sea out of my head – or thought I had. In the year since my father died, I had learned to live without it. It had been hard at first but in the last few months I had given sailing no thought at all.

But it had come back in on a high tide and I knew now that any idea that I could spend my life ashore was a pretence. I was born to be a mariner. It was who I was.

I walked downstairs in darkness and was startled to realise my mother was sitting at the table.

'You had better hurry,' she said in a low voice with no trace of emotion. 'Dawn will be breaking soon. Your uncle has already gone.'

'What do you mean?' I asked.

'I know you will leave one day,' she said. 'I always have. It might as well be today as any other. My heart will break whenever it is.'

'Mother,' I said, tears filling my eyes. 'Please. I won't go. I'll stay with you. I'll stay for ever.'

'No,' she said quietly. 'No, you won't. Go.'

Her words stabbed my heart, but they were true. I said nothing and did not move. My eyes were getting used to the dark and I saw her looking at me, her eyes shimmering darkly.

'Go,' she said again. 'Your uncle will watch out for you. And maybe you can watch out for him.'

She stood up and walked towards me and we hugged in the darkness. I felt a tear drip on to my neck and I wasn't sure whether it was hers or mine.

'Travel,' she said. 'Have your adventures. And then come home to me and meet a girl and settle down and give me grandchildren to play with.'

I got dressed. I packed my father's old kitbag, which he had gifted me the first day I sailed with him. I had no idea what we might face and so I packed everything I could.

'Be prepared for everything and you will stand some chance,' my father had told me once. 'And that's the best you can hope for as a seafaring man.'

My mother had been crying before we embraced in the doorway and she cried again as I held her, and I'm not ashamed to say I shed tears as well. Had the pull of the sea not been so strong, I'd have thrown down my kitbag there and then.

Several times on the way to the harbour, I almost went back. I never turned round once, because I knew that if I caught sight of my mother that would be it, and I would lose all my courage and run home.

I felt as though I shrank as I walked, becoming smaller and smaller as I got nearer and nearer to the ships moored in the bay.

My uncle was standing on the harbour wall
with a group of men. He saw me walking towards
him and took his leave of them.

'You've come to see me off?' he said.

Then he saw my bag.

'I've come to join you,' I said. 'If I can?'

'Aye!' he said with a grin. 'The captain was
saying he was a little short-handed. He'll be glad
to have you.'

He looked past me in the direction of my home.

'Does your mother know?' he asked. 'Only –'

'She knows,' I said.

My uncle looked at me steadily, searching my
face for signs of a lie. When he saw none, he
patted me on the shoulder and ushered me
towards the group of men he had been talking to.

'This is my young nephew,' he said. 'He wants
to serve with you, Captain.'

A short, thick-set man with a leathery face and
wild beard stepped forward.

'Have you sailed before?' he said.

'Aye, sir,' I answered. 'Many times. My father
had his own –'

'Do as I say and we'll get along,' he said.

With that he turned and walked away and my
interview was over. My uncle laughed and clapped
me on the back.

'It's just his way,' he said. 'He's the best, they say.'

'You haven't sailed with him before?'

'No,' said my uncle. 'But I rarely sail with the same captain twice. It's just the way of things. You get to be a good judge of a man, though – and I think we're in safe hands. I have . . .'

He was looking distractedly over my shoulder and, following his gaze, I saw that he was staring at the pilot's son, who was standing on the tide-line some way off, his eyes fixed on my uncle.

'Who is that boy?' asked my uncle.

I told him.

'Don't mind him,' I said. 'He is . . .'

I struggled to find the right words.

'He is different.'

'Different?' said my uncle with a snort. 'Well different or not, I'll not be stared at.'

With that, he set off towards the pilot's son.

'Uncle . . .' I pleaded, chasing after him, fearful of what he might do. I thought the boy would run away, but instead he stood fast and frowned at my uncle as he approached.

'So, the Devil walks among us,' the boy said.

I laughed, but my uncle was clearly not amused.

'There are demons all around him,' he continued. 'They fly about his head and swim in his wake.'

'You dare call me the Devil?' said my uncle, lunging towards him.

I stood in front of him, blocking his way.

'He means no harm,' I said.

'Should I give him leave to call me the Devil, then?' he asked angrily.

'He doesn't know what he's saying.'

My uncle gave me a great shove and pushed me out of the way. I stumbled and fell heavily on to the pebbles.

'Perhaps a thrashing will clear his head.'

'You'd better thrash me first,' said the pilot, trudging towards us along the beach.

Years of rowing a heavy boat in the bay had made the pilot into a man that few would argue with.

'Is this your boy?' asked my uncle, weighing up the opposition.

'It is,' said the pilot.

'Then teach him some manners,' snapped my uncle.

The pilot took a step closer and I thought he was about to strike my uncle down.

'It seems like you are the one who could do with some education in that regard,' said the pilot, putting his arm round his son. 'He's just a harmless boy. Shame on you.'

My uncle was struck by the truth of these words, I could see, though he tried to pretend that he paid no heed. He waved the pilot away and set off towards the harbour. The pilot and his son both watched him go and I, with a nod to them, set off after him.

My uncle's mood did not improve as the crew gathered together in the harbour to be taken to the ship by the pilot and by the time we got into the boat he had become sullen and withdrawn. I feared a repeat of his earlier outburst when the pilot's son climbed into the boat with us and spent the whole time staring at my uncle. But my uncle ignored him.

Perhaps he accepted that the pilot was more important than he was at that moment. And the pilot was important. The bay was wide but dangerously shallow in parts. The pilot knew the channels and would take the helm as we cast off. Without him, few ships would enter or leave the harbour in safety.

I looked back towards the harbour mouth and saw my mother standing at the head of the small crowd gathered on the jetty. I was filled with a terrible mix of feelings as I waved to her. I don't know if she saw me at all, because she did not wave back.

We climbed aboard and hauled anchor. The pilot took the helm and steered our course on the outgoing tide. I turned to look back once more and already we were so far away I could no longer distinguish one figure from the next standing on the jetty and soon I could not see any figures at all. My uncle walked up and put his arm around my shoulder.

'Be of good heart,' he said cheerfully. 'The sea is your mother now, boy.'

We dropped the pilot and his son in the bay and they bade us farewell. As soon as their boat was loose and they were rowing back to shore, we made sail and headed out to sea.

Looking towards the flat horizon, the sea lit by the rosy glow of morning, I thought of the future and of the great adventures before me. My heart fluttered. I had waited for this all my life.

VIII

I wondered why I saw no sign of the rich adventurers my uncle had told us about, but he explained that they were going to follow in another ship.

He had been sent by them to pay the captain to bring this ship. We would join them on the coast of Africa and then cross the rest of the ocean together.

'Their ship will be full of fighting men,' said my uncle. 'I've served with some of them. Good men.'

'Why aren't you on that ship?' I asked.

'They thought it best that they had a presence on this one,' he said. 'Just to make sure we're all rowing in the same direction, so to speak.'

A sailor walked past, and spat on the deck near our feet. My uncle frowned and watched him walk away and disappear out of sight before turning back to me as though nothing had happened.

'They thought it best to have at least one fighting man aboard,' he said, patting his crossbow. 'We may have need of this on the way. The seas are full of pirates.'

'Pirates?' I murmured.

My uncle chuckled.

'Don't you worry about them, lad,' he said. 'I can shoot the eye out of a wasp with this.'

The spitting sailor snorted as he passed once again. My uncle tapped him on the shoulder and he turned round.

'What's your problem?' said my uncle.

The sailor smiled.

'No problem here, friend,' he said. 'Not unless you're thinking of being the cause of one.'

My uncle stepped forward and the sailor's smile disappeared.

'That'll be enough of that,' said the captain, striding towards them. 'And that goes for the rest of you. There'll be no fighting on this ship. Anyone who does will be flogged. No exceptions.'

My uncle and the sailor stared at each other in silence.

'Understood?' said the captain.

'Aye, aye, sir,' said the sailor.

'Aye,' said my uncle, eventually.

My uncle walked away and I saw the captain's eyes narrow as he watched him go. He had the look of a man who saw a storm approaching.

IX

In time we did indeed hit some rough seas off Biscay. I had been out in bad weather before, but nothing like this. I should have been afraid had I not been so excited. What a fool I was then.

As my uncle had promised, the captain was a good one and so was the crew. We were more than a match for the storm we travelled through and we bonded as sailors will in such circumstances.

More to the point, I was not that bad myself. My father had taught me well and I found that busy hands made for a calm mind. I saw my uncle watch me go about my work as though I was an old sea dog, and nod appreciatively. I was proud.

By the time the seas calmed, I felt a kinship with all the men of that ship, as we each of us knew we could trust the man next to us entirely. Trust him with our lives if necessary.

When we didn't work, we talked, and I came to

learn the stories of each man and the many different routes that lead a man down to the sea.

I came to know their characters: who was quick to anger and who was quick to laugh, who liked to tell a tale and who to listen. This was true of all the crew save one: my uncle.

I grew no closer to my uncle than I already had. It wasn't long before I felt more at ease with the cook or the captain than I did with him. They in their turn felt comfortable enough in my presence to tell me in no uncertain terms that they sympathised with me for being related to such a cold and unfriendly man as my uncle.

I could see their point. He stood apart. No one worked harder aboard that ship, or with more skill or knowledge. You could not fault his seamanship. But he made it clear he had no interest in the other men of the crew.

He carried his crossbow with him whenever it was practical to do so, even though it must have weighed him down. He seemed to wear it like a badge, a badge that, in his mind at any rate, set him above all the others. He carried that crossbow all over the ship and would sit, when at rest, cradling it like an infant, or examining it and checking it constantly.

He did talk to the men, but not by way of

normal conversation. When his watch was done and the men gathered to talk and play dice, my uncle would always have a story to tell of his adventures.

The fact that he had largely ignored the others most of the day did not appear to dampen their interest though. He was a good storyteller and the men were glad of the entertainment.

But I could see that, as the nights went on, they grew tired of stories in which my uncle was always the hero – though rarely a valiant one. They grew more sceptical too. If not of the tales, then of my uncle's part in them. So, in time, did I.

Seemingly my uncle had sailed in every major battle of the last twenty years and played a major part in every one. He had travelled everywhere in search of gold and spent what he had managed to find on drink and beautiful women.

The sailors had seen his tattoos as I had and, when asked their meaning, he told them that treasure was often the property of religious houses and these marks were to ward off the bad luck that went with stealing from such places. I thought of the pilot's boy seeing demons around my uncle as he walked to our house.

And then one night something changed. When

he was telling a story about raiding a remote island monastery, one of the listeners interrupted angrily.

'You'd steal from the Church?' he asked.

'Aye,' said my uncle without pause, fingering his cross. 'What business does the Church have in treasure? They should thank me. Greed is a sin. I am saving their souls from damnation.'

My uncle clearly thought this very amusing and laughed heartily. But he was the only one who did. His own laughter dried up and an uncomfortable silence took over, broken only by the angry breathing of those around him.

He seemed to realise he had overstepped some unseen mark, though he had realised too late. The crew had never liked him, and now the first signs of actual *dis*like moved in like a dark cloud.

X

We arrived at the Cape Verde Islands and dropped anchor, loading up with supplies on the quayside at Mindelo. It was the first time I had set foot on foreign soil. I was excited.

Strange trees towered above us and sheltered brightly coloured birds that flitted here and there and pecked at scraps behind the market traders, whose wares were wonderful and strange to my unworldly eyes.

And here it was I saw my first Africans. I had never seen a black face in all my life, but here they were common. Slave ships crowded the harbour and some of the slaves were sold here. We saw them shuffle by: men and women, children too – their ankles and wrists chained in irons. Some had been bought by islanders and they alone toiled in the full searing heat of the sun.

The people here spoke a language I did not understand and which I soon learned was Portuguese.

My uncle surprised me by showing himself to be fluent. He said it paid to know the language of your would-be enemies and he knew a fair amount of Spanish, French, Dutch and Turkish too.

I marvelled to hear him talk to the traders in this strange tongue. I stood there, grinning like a fool, looking from face to face, as he bargained over a stall filled with what I later learned were watermelons. The melon seller used a huge knife to cut us slices and handed them over with a grin filled with gold teeth.

I took a little persuasion to try this strange fruit, but it turned out to be delicious and we sat in the shade spitting pips on the cobbles whilst the captain haggled over our supplies.

The Portuguese soldiers eyed my uncle with suspicion. As always, he had the crossbow on his back, and one of the crew had told me that the soldiers were always on guard against the pirates who regularly attacked the islands. My uncle cared little about this attention or showed no sign of caring if he did. He ignored them. Very soon, he found some shade, settled down and ignored us all.

I joined the others of a younger age from the crew and we explored the area whilst we waited for the captain to call us back to the ship. We looked for lizards on the hot stone walls and stared at the pretty girls who stood in a chattering group in the shade of the church.

We stayed three days at Mindelo, making good the damage the ship had suffered during our voyage there and stocking up on provisions. Mainly though, we were waiting for the other ships – the ships with the sponsors of the expedition. We were to meet here and sail the rest of the journey together.

But by the third day, their ships had still to appear. And my uncle had been right when he told me and my mother about the dangers of leaving a crew idle ashore. The captain had already had to buy the freedom of four men who got into a brawl and rescue another who was in danger of being killed by an angry husband.

At sundown on that third day, the captain gathered the crew on the quayside.

'We have waited long enough for our comrades to arrive,' he said. 'We cannot wait any longer. The food we have on board will perish and we will quickly exhaust what moneys we have buying more from these thieves.'

Here he looked away towards the flock of hawkers and merchants who crowded on the quayside.

'The leader of the expedition ordered me to return home if they have not made contact in three days and, as they have not, back we go,' he said.

'I was told of no such plan,' said my uncle.

'Well, then,' said the captain, 'perhaps they did not feel it of vital importance to tell you.'

There was a ripple of laughter at my uncle's expense.

'Are we simply to abandon the expedition then?' he said. 'I thought you were made of stronger stuff.'

'It would be insanity to continue,' said the captain. 'What purpose would be served? We are one ship, a supply ship. Without the others we are nothing. I am not taking these men to the Pacific for sport. I have a letter from my employers. Here.'

The captain handed my uncle a letter. He read it quickly and handed it back.

'I say again,' he said. 'I was not informed of –'

'You've been informed now!' said the captain angrily.

The sailors nearby smiled and chuckled and muttered as they moved away to row back to the ship. I turned to look at my uncle. He stood alone, holding the cross around his neck, his face a picture of rage.

We stayed at anchor that last night. There was a strange atmosphere. We had gone very quickly from the fearful excitement of heading into the unknown, to the knowledge that we were now to sail home, back to our loved ones. I thought of my mother and wished that I could wake up back in my own bed. If we were not to sail on, I wanted to be home right away.

I was not alone in this, I soon discovered, once the men were below and talking. If there was no adventure ahead, then we were all for a fair wind to take us home as speedily as possible.

I think I was the only one who voiced any disappointment at having the voyage cut short. An old sailor slapped his big hand on my back and said there'd be plenty more voyages ahead.

I smiled and hoped he was right and looked to my uncle. But he was off in the shadows alone, polishing the wood of his crossbow and greasing the metalwork. We all flinched at the click of the trigger as he tested it and I saw his white smile glowing in the darkness.

XI

The storm, when it came, flew like a banshee out of the west and struck us full in the face. We were not more than a couple of hours out of port.

I thought the storm we had sailed through in the Bay of Biscay was bad, but it was a gentle breeze compared to this tempest. And it hit with such speed. We saw it on the horizon, and then it was upon us.

I had been sent aloft to trim the sails and I was forced to cling to the spar with all my might. The rain greased the wood and the wind seemed to pull purposefully, spitefully, at my fingers, trying to prise them free.

Two men were plucked from the topsails: one thrown into the crashing waves to drown, the other hurled headlong to the deck, dashing out his brains. The ship swung this way and that. One moment the spar tips would be skimming the wave crests as we leaned so far that I felt most surely we were bound to capsize and all of us drown; then the ship would take the waves head on, climbing with the prow skyward, the deck tipped back, throwing all towards the stern. Then there would be a heart-stopping moment of stillness as the ship crested the wave and crashed down over the other side, the prow ramming the next wave with such force that it lifted the stern clear of the water, hurling us all towards the prow.

The noise was deafening. The roar of the wind and the sea and the constant attack of the rain on our heads engulfed the voices of the men, who I could see were shouting out. Each of us, old and young, looked to our allotted tasks and did them the best we could. Our lives depended on it.

But more lives were lost all the same. I was working in the topsails when three men were washed overboard to be swallowed up by the ravenous waters. I saw them rise up atop a giant wave and then sink into its hungry darkness.

I thought about what the hermit had once told me. He said the sea was one huge living creature. If that was true, we had encountered the ravening mouth and teeth. Three more men were swept overboard and devoured, one of them the old mariner who had told me I had many more voyages ahead. It didn't feel that way.

The sea was by turns black and dark green and slate grey, and it rose up like a range of mountains stretching into the distance. I had never seen the like of it. After a while, I had to stop looking into those waves, for it was as though I looked into the doom of the world.

The sky closed in around us: if I'd reached out my hand I could almost have touched the soot-black clouds that swirled about the topsails. Sea and sky, sky and sea – it all melded into one.

The storm flew past us and then turned about, chasing us from behind. It threw us forward and, though the helmsman did his best to steer, the storm was our pilot now. We went wherever the winds decided and we were spun about so many times none of us knew whether we were heading north or south, east or west.

I saw the look of panic and despair written on the faces of older sailors who had seen storms before. They too had seen nothing like this. Any little pause in the storm's roaring and all I could hear was the mumbled prayers of every man around me.

I heard one man pray that the ship go down quick if it was going. My father had told me never to learn to swim. 'If your ship goes down,' he had said, 'better to go down quick with it than to float about on the surface, waiting to die of thirst or be taken bit by bit by hungry sharks.'

So I'd never learned. Nor had most of the men on the ship, I'd have wagered. Most thought it was bad luck. Learning to swim was like saying you thought the ship was going to sink. But that is what everyone now thought, regardless.

The storm punched us and punched us until we were drunk with it, and then it punched some more. The whole ship reeled and everyone aboard staggered dizzily about, exhausted and battered.

I began to imagine what it would be like, slipping beneath the waves, sucking water into my lungs instead of air – down, down into the blackness until there was nothing. I was so tired that such a prospect didn't strike me as so very bad. In any case, I think we all felt it was only a matter of time.

I remember a wave rising up so high it seemed to be higher than the top of the mainmast and it was as black as ink. It was like a great shadow. It rose up like a giant and towered over the ship before crashing down, swamping the deck and flinging the crew this way and that as though we were cod hauled up and let loose on a wet deck.

I heard men talking and saying that we must be being driven west and that we would end up in the Americas, like it or not, for that was where these storms were determined to drive you when they hit.

'We'll end up in the Bermudas, mark my words,' shouted one, over the raging wind.

'Well, there's worse places to be forced ashore!' bellowed another. 'Plenty of beautiful women there, and plenty of rum too!'

The captain ordered half the crew to rest and they went below to try to sleep. By the time our shift was relieved, I was almost asleep myself, holding on to a thick hemp rope for dear life, so I wouldn't get washed overboard.

We staggered below deck and collapsed into our hammocks as best we could. Despite the noise and bucking of the ship, exhaustion overtook me and I slept, awakened every few minutes by the din and the wild motion.

The storm continued in my sleep. The waves of my dreams were even larger, our ship even smaller. And stranger still, my uncle stood at the storm's eye, whether directing it or whether the sole target of its venom, it was hard to tell.

XII

Day after day, night after night, the storm raged. Then one morning I woke unsure of where I was. I leapt to my feet in alarm, not knowing why I was so unnerved, and then realised that the ship no longer lurched and rolled. So strange was this calmness that I rushed on deck to see what was happening.

At first I was overjoyed. I grinned as I leapt each rung of the ladder and bounced on deck. We'd survived the tempest! It should have been a cause for celebration. But I found a sombre gathering of the crew.

The men stood in silent stillness, so removed from the frantic activity I'd known in the previous days. It was an eerie sight – and a strange glimpse of the horror to come.

The sea was now calm, as was the air above and around us. A thick mist wrapped itself about us, and it was fiercely cold.

There should have been thanks given for being saved from the storm, but we were all too perplexed by our new situation to give any thought to anything but the fogbound present.

Had we been driven north? Were we now back in the cold climes of our own country? But, no, the captain informed us that, as much as he could be sure of anything, he was certain that somehow we had been driven south, and at such an unnatural speed that we had crossed the equator without knowing it. We had arrived in the chill waters that lie at the far end of the Atlantic near the very straits we'd been originally bound for: the straits that would see us sail into the Pacific Ocean.

But how, in the space of one night, could we have drifted into waters so cold? How could the climate change so swiftly? I looked to older faces for the answer but there was none. It was a wonder to them all.

My uncle stood apart as usual, a scowl on his face as though the storm lingered on in his person. He leaned on his crossbow and stared malevolently at the deck.

The damp air soaked our clothes and all the crew were soon chilled to the bone. I began to shiver and found that I couldn't stop. My teeth rattled in my head and the joints of my arms and legs knocked one against the other until they ached.

It took an effort of will to persuade my legs to take me back below deck so that I could grab my father's winter coat. I hugged myself and stamped away the cold as he had taught me to. Then I put on his old mittens and came back on deck to hear the captain's orders.

They gave no comfort. He told us that whatever fog we were in seemed to have some hold over the compass because the needle spun and spun and would not tell us which way to go. We could see neither sun nor stars through the mist. We were lost and had no notion of which way we were headed.

The captain ordered some of us – and I was one – to go up into the topsails and act as lookouts. We were to watch for land or for other ships – anything that might help us get a bearing on where we were.

I climbed the wet rigging of the main channels, high, high up into the airy top of the mainmast and clambered into the crow's-nest.

I leaned over and looked down. The mist was so thick all about that I could scarcely see the deck, as when on deck, the top of the mast seemed to be disappearing into the cloud.

I realised straight away that I was going to be of little use to the captain up there. I would see nothing until we were practically on top of it. Any land I saw, the ship would almost certainly run aground on before the sound of my voice had travelled down to the deck.

But, in any event, I saw nothing. It was so featureless I could hardly tell if the ship was even moving, though I knew she must be because the breeze chilled my face and swelled the sails.

The mist hung about me and soaked me through and through. I stared out on to the greyness, barely able to see the next mast. Suddenly, out of the mist loomed a massive cliff face and the whole crew cried out in terror. We looked set to run aground on some strange frozen island and the helmsman threw the wheel with all his might.

No sooner had we avoided this icy crag than another loomed up to take its place – and another. It was as though we had blundered into an archipelago and were surrounded by islands, each more treacherous than the next.

But these were not islands. Leastwise they weren't islands of rock; they were floating islands of ice. Some of the crew had seen their like before in the frozen north, though none had ventured this far south and could never have guessed that we might find icebergs here.

I was relieved at first when I heard they were merely huge chunks of ice. My fear had been we would run aground on one of these sharp reefs. But I was a fool of course. These icebergs could crush a ship like tinder. They were mountains that only showed their peaks whilst the great body of them was beneath the surface.

Sure enough, the ship's hull squealed as it scraped along the ragged edge of one of these monsters. The noise was deafening. It was terrifying too. It sounded like nothing I had ever heard in my life till then. It was like a thousand demons shrieking.

I clamped my hands to my ears to shut it out and saw I wasn't the only one. Then the mist parted momentarily and we saw, to our horror, that the ocean all about was studded with the peaks of icebergs, drifting in the currents like the deathly fins of giant white sharks.

The captain was the first to come to his senses and ordered every man who was not otherwise occupied to grab a pole of any kind and climb the sides to push at any iceberg that came close.

I climbed down, grabbed a pole and hauled myself over the bulwarks to stand on the mainstays, where the great ropes from the main-masts fixed themselves to the hull.

With my left arm hooked upon the rigging and my feet fighting for purchase on the slippery, ice-coated wooden board and ropes, I held the pole like a jousting knight and pushed with all my might.

It felt good to be doing something, but in truth we all knew that our lives were in the hands of the fates now. Any one of these ice fangs might rip out the guts of the ship and down we'd go into those freezing waters.

The mist rolled back in again. It was frightening because of what it concealed from our eyes. It made us feel as though we were floating through cloud, flying almost. It was dizzying, not being able to see anything around us at all. Far, far worse, though, were those moments when the mist parted and we could see our icy hell.

Eventually there was more ice than ocean and the very sea froze. I couldn't believe my eyes. How could the sea freeze? I was sure such a thing was not possible. And yet slowly but surely our ship was becoming surrounded by ice – more and more spikes of ice standing up out of the water as though the sharks were circling us, ready for the kill.

Snow fell through the mist, gently at first but soon steadily. It coated the deck. It coated the sea as well until the sea seemed to be stiffening into a kind of icy porridge.

The dirty white crust rose and fell in the wake of the ship whilst the snowfall got heavier and heavier and the air got colder and colder.

Soon the sea was white, and instead of a thin scum, the ice was now a thick crust that cracked and splintered as the ship forced its way through.

The snow was frosting the ice sheet forming around the ship, until everything: the ship, the sea – was deathly pale in every direction. Never in my worse nightmares had I ever imagined a world so dreadful. It was as though everything was dissolving into this nothing.

Though this was nothing to what lay ahead.

The ice became thicker still and the ship began to slow. This grinding to a halt was made to the sound of more ear-splitting growls and squeals and moans as the ice squeezed in on the timbers of the hull. We knew that at any moment, the ice would win its battle with the wood and the hull would be crushed.

The ship became still. The growling gradually died away and we were encased in ice. The world was almost silent once again, apart from the eerie whistling of a breeze playing among the rigging. Snow and ice had smothered us. Icicles hung from the spars, snow carpeted the deck. Men stood like frozen meat, staring dumbfounded into the white horror, their breath rising up in tiny bursts of steam.

XIII

No sailor alive doesn't think about his death. I had imagined many kinds of death: some ordinary – drowning at sea like my poor father or being crushed against the rocks of some reef; some more elaborate – cooked by cannibals or butchered by pirates. Not once had I ever imagined that I would simply freeze to a statue in some icy hell.

On the second day in the ice, I came up from the hold to find that the layer of snow on the deck had frozen solid. The snow no longer fell as before, but if anything it was even colder than it had been the previous night when I had lain shivering, trying to sleep.

When I say 'night', I should add that this word did not have the same meaning here, because although we could not see the sun through the mist, we could tell that it had never quite set.

Instead of the certainty of night, there was the

odd halfway house of twilight – a twilight that lasted for hours and hours without ever slipping into darkness. It all just added to the feeling we had that we had fallen into some frozen netherworld.

A man who had slept near me stood gazing out into the mist so steadily that I walked up to ask him if he had seen something. He made no reply and did not move when I nudged him.

I leaned round to look at his face and saw it was a horrible blueish purple. His eyes were open and tiny icicles hung from his lashes. His very tears were frozen and I could see the veins in the eyeballs where the blood too was doubt- less frozen. They had to break his fingers to release the grip he had on the rope he stood beside.

He was the first to die of the cold, but not the last. I thanked God that I had brought warm clothing, for it was those among us who had none who fell victim to the chill. The bodies were taken off the ship and left out on the ice. They were dragged some distance away – just far enough to be, mercifully, shrouded by the fog.

I left the ship myself on one of these 'burials', helping to dispose of the corpse of a one-eyed man from the north country. He was a big man with a booming laugh – or had been in life – and it took three of us to carry him down the side of the ship and drag him across the ice.

Whilst the other two untied the rope we had bound about him to pull him along, I stood and marvelled at the fact that we were standing on water turned to rock. In harsh winters, I had seen ice form on puddles and horse-troughs and buckets, but the notion that it could be this thick and over such a distance – it was as though the whole world was frozen. At that moment I had no way of knowing that it wasn't.

This thought seemed to seep into my bones as an extra layer of chill and I stood staring into the mist as the others left the body and returned to the ship.

The only sound was the crunch of the retreating footsteps on the ice, but as that died away I was sure that there were other sounds – sounds so faint that I could hardly hear them.

They were muffled even further by the fleece hat I wore. If I moved my head even slightly, the sounds disappeared. I strained to make sense of them as my uncle walked up to me.

'What is it?' he said.

'Shhh,' I said, pointing into the mist. 'Don't you hear that?'

My uncle peered into the blankness and leaned forward, tilting his head like a bird. He nodded.

'Aye,' he said.

'What do you think it –'

'Whispering . . .'

As soon as he said it, I knew it was true. The sound was of many voices whispering – whether quietly or far away, it was impossible to tell. My stomach lurched as I had the impression of a great horde of unseen spirits standing just beyond the curtain of the mist, watching us and whispering to each other.

I couldn't hear anything of what they said, only the sound of the breath on their lips. My uncle took a step forward, leaning out and cocking his head like a bird again, but checked himself. I could see the fear in his face that must have shown in mine. And I had never seen fear in his face before. Not once.

'Let's get back,' he said, suddenly turning round and heading off towards the ship.

I could not have stayed a moment more alone there on the ice. As I walked away, the voices seemed to get a little louder, although still they never reached anything but a low murmur, like the wind playing in the dry leaves of a far away forest.

As chilling as it had been to face these hidden voices, it was a hundred times more frightening to turn our backs on them. I lowered my eyes to the ice and concentrated on following my uncle's footsteps.

XIV

Back at the ship, that whispering was always there, behind all the other sounds. Once heard, it seemed to latch itself on and not let go.

And the others heard it too. During the working part of the day it was easier to block it out. As I lay trying to sleep through the bitter cold, the sound would come creeping back into my head from out of the silence.

I thought of the hermit and the pilot's boy and the demons he said that he saw swimming in the air around my uncle. Was it those demons I could hear? Or were we going as crazy as the pilot's boy?

I thought too of the hermit and his story about the man who thought we lived a dream and wondered if this was what this was. Were we all living in a dream, a nightmare? Were we all actors in a world of my uncle's making?

The despair of the crew was intense. It was far worse than the fear in the storm. Fear is something you can fight. Despair is like a vampire, draining your energy.

It was horrible to see. Some of those men must have witnessed terrible things. Some had been shipwrecked, I knew. And if only a tiny part of my uncle's tales were true, then he had seen things that would have sent me running and screaming. And yet this whispering mist had defeated the crew. They had given up. You could see it in their eyes.

And then it came. Out of the mist like a dove, like the Holy Spirit from a church painting. It glowed like it was lit by some light it carried with it – white and pure against the dull and dismal mist.

But this bird was no dove. It was huge. It soared on wings wider than the span of a man's arms. It soared with barely a flap of those wings, though hardly a breath of a breeze blew. It wheeled about the ship with scarcely a wingbeat.

One by one, each man stopped and watched. You could have traced the flight path by the movement of their faces. They were like flowers following the sun.

We called to it – more and more of us, until the whole crew shouted out. It was good to break that wretched stillness. We were so cheered to see some kind of life in that barren place. Grown men's eyes filled with tears and those tears froze on their cheeks.

This place – this dreadful, desolate place we had become trapped in – was empty of life and of the sense that any living creature had ever been there or could ever live there. And yet here was this bird.

We had seen nothing but each other since the onset of the storm that chased us to this hell. And we were no comfort at all. The cold and boredom were making madmen of us all and we had, day by day, become less and less human. We shuffled about slowly, scarcely uttering a word.

The bird sweeping in like that was like a peal of church bells or the sun bursting through clouds or a great roar of laughter. Life. That's what it was. Something was alive in this world and it lifted our hearts and took our minds away from the creeping horror of the ice and the mist.

Every frozen, gaunt and beaten face I could see smiled on that bird and I looked to my uncle to see whether even he might wear a grin, but my view of him was blocked.

'Albatross,' said a man nearby.

'Aye,' said another. 'I've seen them before. They can fly for days and never land.'

The man turned to me to explain.

'They fly over the waves,' he said. 'Skimming them with their wing tips. They are a beautiful sight to see and that's for sure.'

The albatross seemed to hear the man and down it came, skimming the frozen waters and then rising up again to swoop across the deck and through the rigging and up to the tops of the masts.

We cheered as heartily as though we were at the theatre or the bear-baiting pit. Men turned to each other and pointed and clapped. The bird was putting on a show for us and we loved it.

Then, to everyone's amazement, the albatross's circling of the ship got lower and tighter and all at once it swept in and landed on the deck, the men clearing a space for it as it skidded to a halt.

It strolled in an ungainly fashion, completely at odds with the grace of its flight, and this only served to make us love it more. It was as comical as a goose as it waddled round the deck and we chuckled to see it.

In the air it had seemed a distant thing, but now it walked among us and we took it straight away to our hearts. All of us, at once. Or so I thought.

One of the crew, a good-natured joker from the Welsh mountains, stepped forward holding out a piece of salt cod. The crew clucked and murmured encouragement, like children trying to coax a kitten.

The albatross clicked its beak and cocked his head and waddled over to peck the morsel from his fingers. It tested it for a moment, then swallowed it whole. You could see it going down its neck.

'Want some more?' asked the sailor, and the albatross nodded its head in response. We all laughed and the albatross flinched at the noise and jumped back.

'Put the food away, you fool!' said a gruff voice behind me which I recognised immediately to be that of my uncle.

The crew – and the albatross too – turned as one to face him, the smiles slipping from their faces. My uncle stepped forward, holding his crossbow. I saw that it was loaded.

'Put the food away,' he repeated.

'I give the orders on this ship,' said the captain, pushing his way through. 'And I'll thank you to put that weapon down.'

My uncle did not move and did not take his eyes from the albatross. I turned to look at the captain. Then my uncle spoke again.

'We are God knows where,' he said, as though talking to fools. 'When was the last time we saw land? What man here can say when it will next be that we can go ashore and take food on board? Or even if there be any food in this place? I'll wager that –'

'I said put the crossbow down!' shouted the captain.

My uncle stared, his mouth still part-way open from speaking, his eyes narrowed to a fierce scowl. Slowly, he lowered the crossbow. The captain walked over to where he stood and looked him in the face.

'If you ever again point that thing at any man aboard my ship, I will toss it in the sea and hang you from the yardarm. Do I make myself clear?'

'Aye, captain,' said my uncle after a pause.

The captain walked away and the men, after a while, returned to their previous high spirits and continued their attentions to the albatross.

My uncle stood alone, staring at them, the crossbow still loaded and cocked. I was the only one who looked at him. I was the only one who saw the look of madness in his eyes.

XV

The albatross came back every day and every day was greeted like a friend. And a good friend is what it turned out to be. The ice that had held us in its choking grip now began to crack and splinter.

As the albatross flew above our heads, the ice sheet gave out a loud groan and shattered. The ship lurched forward like a penned pony whose gate had just been opened.

Round and round, the albatross flew, its wide wings white against the black sky. It circled about the mainmast as though tied to the crow's nest, and with each revolution the ice seemed to weaken.

Instead of a flat white plain, the ice sheet was now riven with cracks and the ship was floating free again, albeit still as yet trapped in chains of broken ice.

It took a while to sink in, but then a great roar went up and we hugged one another and jumped up and down, laughing and clapping each other on the back. There was a new warmth in the air. It began to melt the ice covering the ship, and icicles began to rain down on the deck, shattering into tiny twinkling fragments.

Sailors are a superstitious tribe and we were sure that the albatross was some spirit sent to help us. It couldn't be a coincidence, could it? The bird had come; the ice had gone. There could only be one explanation.

This belief became only more devout when a breeze began to blow and grow and turn into a wind that filled the sails and puffed them out proudly. We cheered as the helmsman steered a course through the shattered ice floe.

Only my uncle refused to join this celebration of the bird. He could see there was little point in arguing as he was in a minority of one. It was clear from his face that his opinion of the albatross and the devotion of the crew had not changed.

I did not care. The bird was hope and I wanted hope. We headed north and left those seas of ice behind us. Each day the icebergs grew more scarce until, one day, the sea was entirely free of their wretched presence. I had almost forgotten what the wild free ocean looked like.

The albatross stayed with us. It was like it wanted to guide us safely home and I know that every man aboard – save for my uncle – prayed that it might never leave us, though I suppose we knew it must.

Those who were not working ignored their usual sports and stood calling up to the bird, beckoning it down until, eventually, the albatross seemed to give in to their requests and descended like an angel to join them and accept whatever scraps they offered.

It was so tame now that it would take the food from our hands and even permit us to touch its head. Nevertheless we were always respectful of the creature. I myself felt the fine feathers on its head and thought myself as blessed for doing so as had I been touching a holy relic.

I looked into its dark, kind eyes. It calmed me. For that moment all my worries and fears melted away.

But when I turned away, I saw my uncle standing in the shadow of the mainmast. I will never forget the look on his face. The madness I had noted days before seemed now to have seeped into his whole body. He simmered with it, like a scalding hot iron waiting to be touched by an unwary hand.

Perhaps I could have changed things then. Perhaps I should have run to the captain and spoken to him. Yet he was my uncle after all and, besides, how could I have known what he was about to do? In any case, I wonder if our fates were already mapped out.

XVI

I said nothing to the captain, out of loyalty to my uncle. I still had the ties of kinship with him but I certainly would never have sought out his company. Yet still I didn't want to be the cause of any trouble to him.

We sailed on, all of us happy to pretend that nothing was now amiss – that all would be well in time so long as we could see the next few days out with the albatross as our mascot and guide.

This was not a simple thing, for although the ice was gone the mist remained, and though the ship was driven by a healthy breeze this breeze seemed not to have any influence on the terrible mist.

So on we sailed, blind beyond a few hundred yards, unable to see any horizon, wondering if the first thing we would see would be the jagged island or reef we wrecked ourselves upon.

If that uncertainty wasn't bad enough, then the mist itself was terrible in its own right, for that whispering was always there in the background, however much we tried to shut it out. We knew it was an enchanted fog, and we knew that until we were free of it, we were not free of the curse that had pulled us south into the ice.

With this dread of the mist and what it meant always present, the younger of the crew, like me, were especially happy to see the albatross and always first to try to offer it some food whenever it came to rest aboard the ship. The captain didn't shoo us back to work as he might have been expected to do, but understood the mood of his crew and went with it.

The older sailors who had seen this breed of bird before marvelled at this behaviour. They swore they had never ever seen the creatures land before, let alone come to a sailor's call.

We felt blessed. We felt that this bird would be the key to our escape from the enchantment. And then, one day, as I was standing looking up at the albatross, I realised someone was next to me and, turning round, I saw my uncle.

His face was now so gaunt and his eyes so sunken that he was like a pale spectre of his earlier self. I flinched when I looked him in the face and he smiled wryly at my reaction.

'Fear not,' he said.

'I'm not afraid,' I replied, not altogether convincingly. 'I was startled, that's all.'

My uncle nodded and looked up at the albatross wheeling over our heads.

'I'm sorry that we haven't spoken much lately,' I said.

He nodded again without taking his eyes from the bird. As soon as the words had left my mouth, I regretted them. I wasn't sorry at all that I had not spoken to him, and he could tell that from my voice.

'Never mind,' he said. 'It matters not.'

He shook his head and smiled. It was something of his old wolfish smile and it cheered me to see it.

''Tis my fault, lad,' he said. 'I have been ill-humoured and out of sorts. I'm restless. Some men – like your father – love the sailing life, but I am only a mariner to travel to other lands. I care nothing for the sea. The sea is just the road to where I want to be.'

I nodded – not because I agreed, but because I understood what he meant. I felt something in between these two extremes. I had a burning curiosity to see new worlds, and I also had a great urge to know the sea as well as these old mariners, as well as my father.

'I long for a fight,' he said. 'I know where I am in a battle.'

I smiled. He sounded so contented at this thought. The mist seemed to have closed in a little more and I was glad of the distraction.

'Please don't wish that on us,' I said. 'I'll be content with a safe passage home.'

'There was this one time,' he said, ignoring me entirely, 'we were in the mountains near Trebizond on the Black Sea. We had heard of a heathen temple there that had a casket so encrusted with diamonds that it hurt the eyes to look at it, even by candlelight.'

I eased back and let the story wash over me, trying to concentrate on my uncle's words and not the whispering that seemed to have grown in volume as the mist rolled in around us.

'But two days into our journey,' he continued, 'we were ambushed by a bandit king who captured us and told us that the following day at the sun's highest point he would skin us all alive.

'We managed to escape and, though the others were all for running away, I put the case for teaching that heathen a lesson. In the end I managed to persuade them that, if we did not, he would surely catch us, since they were on horse and we on foot.

'We approached at night. They were nomads and his camp was a collection of domed tents, with a makeshift paddock where they kept their horses. There was a full moon and all was going well. We had mounted such attacks before and those men could walk on a carpet of dry twigs without making a sound. But suddenly a sentry saw us and reached for his horn.

'I had one bolt left and knew that it must be a death shot. Anything less and the man would raise the alarm. I had no time to aim and only one chance. Without another thought I just lifted the crossbow and –'

'You and your crossbow,' said a sailor nearby. 'Day after day, polishing it and oiling it and hugging it like it was your wife. Tale upon tale about how you can shoot through the eye of a needle. Enough! All these weeks and we've never seen you fire the damned thing except with your lying mouth.'

The movement was so rapid that I did not see his trigger finger move once the crossbow was raised to his eye, and no one could have stopped him even if we had known his intent. My uncle was every bit as good a shot as he'd said, curse him.

PART THE SECOND

XVII

A terrible silence followed the thud of the albatross hitting the deck. All heads turned to the sound and each face froze in horror at the sight of the bird they had come to love lying stretched out on the boards, its mighty wings flat against the deck.

I pushed myself forward and stared at the pathetic sight. It seemed smaller somehow in death. The joy it had given was gone and the gloom that replaced it worse for coming after it.

We mourned that bird as if it had been a parent or a child. The sadness was like a great weight that slowly descended on us.

But it was not until the captain stepped forwards and turned the bird over that the cross-bow bolt was seen, sticking out of its chest, the feathers dark with blood.

A murmuring rose up and all faces turned towards my uncle. Several men strode towards him and overpowered him, then dragged him towards the captain, who stood near the albatross. The captain pointed at the fallen bird.

'Is this your work?' he said, his eyes half closed, his lips trembling, as though talking to my uncle disgusted him.

My uncle did not answer.

'Speak, damn your eyes!' said the captain. 'I want to hear it from your own lips before I hang you! Did you do this?'

'Hang me?' snarled my uncle, struggling against the men who held him. 'On whose authority? Since when did the killing of a bird become a hanging offence?'

'This is my ship,' said the captain, his face crimson red and his eyes bulging. 'Don't tell me what I can and cannot do.'

'No!' said my uncle, struggling again. 'I'll not hang for the killing of a bird.'

'Who is going to stop me?' said the captain, looking round the crew. 'Who will speak for you?'

My uncle did not turn to me nor did he call me. No one looked at me. And yet I felt as though by staying silent I shouted out at the top my voice, 'Kill him! Hang him!'

They say that blood is thicker than water, but

in that instance I had more fellow feeling for that dead albatross than I had for my uncle. I wished with all my heart that he had never walked into my life.

No one spoke. In fact, no one seemed to breathe for fear that an exhaled breath might be seen as some sign of an objection. But there was to be no objection.

'Lang,' said the captain, 'fetch some rope and make a noose.'

My uncle renewed his struggles but there were too many men holding him. He stamped on someone's foot, and the ship's carpenter stepped forward and hit him in the stomach with one of his huge fists.

'Be still,' he said. 'Tie his hands.'

My uncle gasped and winced and spat on the floor, but he made no further attempt to escape. Where could he escape to, in any case?

The rope was fetched and knotted and someone was sent to tie the other end to the yardarm. The noose was passed down and down until it dangled above my uncle's head. He looked at it and cursed loudly.

The captain fetched my uncle's crossbow, which was still lying on the deck where he had dropped it. I thought perhaps he had changed his mind and was intending to shoot my uncle rather than hang him.

Instead, he lifted it over his head and crashed it against the mast with such force that the whole crew flinched. The crossbow shattered into several pieces that scattered across the deck.

The captain stared at the pieces for a moment, took a deep breath and sighed.

'Fetch that barrel,' he said.

A barrel was grabbed and turned and rolled over towards my uncle and the group who held him. It was righted and set down beneath the noose.

'Get him up,' said the captain.

'No!' shouted my uncle. 'You have no right!'

'When the noose is round your neck,' said the captain wearily, ignoring him, 'I will kick the barrel away and I'll do my best to kick it hard and quick so you might break your neck, but I can't promise anything. Do you have any last words?'

My uncle stared at the captain, his eyes twitching back and forth.

'May you all rot in hell!' he hissed.

'I think we already are,' said the captain. 'Put a hood over his head. I don't want to see his face when he chokes.'

A bag was fetched and roughly hauled over my uncle's face and muffled curses rang out from under it. The group holding him lifted up his legs and tried to get his feet on to the barrel, but he kicked the barrel over.

'Tie his legs,' said the captain. 'If he kicks after that, then break them.'

More rope was fetched and two men went about tying his ankles together. When they were finished, they tried again to get my uncle up on top of the righted barrel.

But just as they were doing this, I noticed something incredible. It was so incredible that I did not even grasp at first the full meaning of what I was seeing. And I was not the only one.

'Wait!' shouted the captain, as the carpenter was about to kick the barrel away. 'Look!'

Many of us were already looking at the shadow of the noose swaying on the deck, and the shadow of my uncle beneath it. Every face was a portrait of amazement. The mist had gone!

The sailors dropped my uncle to the deck and he scurried backwards on his backside until he reached the side of the ship.

But we ignored him now entirely. We were all gazing at the wonderful view of open ocean and wide horizon, the cloud-flecked blue sky and bright sun.

Every heart lifted at the sight. We forgot all about the albatross and all thoughts of executing its killer. We were too happy to let such terrible thoughts into our heads. We were free. Truly free. We had escaped the curse at last.

It was like being blind for years and then having your sight given back in a second. It was some time before I remembered my uncle, who had shuffled away from his would-be killers and was huddled at the far end of the ship, the hood now only partially covering his face.

The captain started to rally the crew to get to work and, taking a knife from a sheath on his waist, he walked over to my uncle and cut the ropes that bound his wrists and ankles.

My uncle snatched the hood from his face and looked up at the captain and the other members of the crew who, like me, had started to wander across to where he lay.

'Get up,' said the captain. 'No man shall harm you. If they do, they shall answer to me.'

'Why?' asked my uncle, looking suspiciously from face to face.

'We are free of the mist,' said the captain.

My uncle peered up at the sky, blinking, clearly

not having noticed until the captain pointed it out.

'It is a day for celebration not killing. Be thankful.'

'Be thankful?' said my uncle. 'You would have hanged me without a care. And now you –'

'I'm sure I can find some men to toss you overboard if you want,' said the captain. 'Thank your lucky stars that we are in better spirits and keep your peace.'

The captain turned away and started giving orders. The crew jumped to their tasks with an enthusiasm that spoke of their days of boredom and belied the weakness that they all felt through lack of food and discomfort.

Eventually it was just me and my uncle. When his eyes met mine, I could not hold his gaze and climbed gratefully when the captain ordered me to the topsails. To be up there with the sun and the wind and the white sails billowing! I felt reborn.

XVIII

I made no further effort to seek out my uncle. At first I felt disloyal, but very quickly I felt nothing at all. I told myself that his troubles were of his own making and there was nothing to be gained by my taking sides with him.

Occasionally he would emerge from the hold as though stepping out of his own tomb, each time looking paler and thinner and less like the man I had known at the start of the voyage, less like a man at all.

The disgust of the rest of the crew was so strong you could feel it in the air. But my uncle seemed not to notice. Or, if he did notice, he made sure not to show it. It was as if the crew had actually killed him and he was haunting them. He was a constant reminder of the loss of the albatross and of their own murderous rage.

But the sun shone after so many days of grey mist. The effect of its rays on the crew was startling to see. The sullenness evaporated along with every trace of moisture in the ship.

It had been so long since we had glimpsed the world unfiltered through the fog that it seemed newly made. Every grain of the timbers stood out in pin-sharp detail. Muted colours now gleamed. The sails hurt your eyes to look at them, they were so bright.

The mood of the ship lifted and the breeze become a good strong wind at our backs. It slapped against the canvas of the mainsails and made the rigging creak and twang like fiddle strings as they fought to rein it in. Foam scudded on the wave crests.

The temperature began to climb and climb with the clear air. The ice world and mist seemed quickly to be a thing of the past. The wet timbers of the ship began to steam and layers of clothing were shed one by one.

Our pleasure at being under blue skies was not strained by the uncomfortable heat. We had only to recall the freezing cold or the creeping, whispering mist and any heat seemed bearable when it came out of clear bright skies.

The sunshine warmed us through, right through – even to our very hearts – and for the first time in what seemed an age a song broke out and we all joined in. Whatever dangers these oceans had to offer, they might be good sailor's dangers – dangers we knew and could battle with. Or so we hoped.

I was singing out with gusto if not much melody when I saw my uncle emerging from the blackness of the hold into the shadow of the mainsail, and he seemed like some left-over particle of the gloom and ice we had escaped.

One by one the men around me saw him too, and as each man saw him they stopped singing as I had done, and, as they stopped, others further off stopped too and craned their necks to try to glimpse what it was that had caused the song to falter.

I did not know what reaction there would be to my uncle's appearance, but never in the world did I think that the captain would step forward and clap him on the back. My uncle flinched, preparing for another lynching.

'Now then, lads,' said the captain to the crew. 'What's done is done and we are safely into open waters. Let's all be glad and let bygones be bygones. What do you say?'

This was greeted by silence and most of the men had their eyes cast down, studying the deck.

But after a while, one by one, they muttered in agreement. There seemed to be no stomach now for any bad feeling. No one wanted to jinx our new good fortune with ill thoughts. Luck could be curdled by such things; every sailor knew it.

This didn't mean that my uncle was carried round the ship shoulder high. He was still mostly ignored – because the crew no doubt harboured feelings of guilt and shame about what they had been about to do.

We all went about our work as the fine breeze filled our sails and hope filled our hearts. Gradually, hour by hour, my uncle, working alongside them, was accepted back into the crew on equal terms. And not just when we worked.

The men began to nod at him when he walked past. They did not deliberately walk away from him as they had before. They would even choose to sit beside him occasionally. They were trying, in their way, to make amends.

It may have begun as a grudging forgiveness but it soon became more – much more. No one looks for meaning in signs and portents as keenly as a mariner. And it had not escaped anyone's notice that moments after the albatross was shot, the fearful mist had dissolved and we were blown into good clear seas and open skies.

Perhaps the albatross had been a demon in disguise. Perhaps it had cast a spell over the crew to distract them from their fate.

'Who's to say that the albatross wasn't keeping us in that mist?' said a sailor standing in a group beside me one day.

'You've changed your tune,' said another.

'No,' said yet another, pushing forward. 'He's right. Our luck changed when the bird was killed.'

'Aye,' said the first. 'I think maybe that bird was some kind of evil spirit. Something that had us bewitched.'

A huge mariner from the far north of Scotland smacked his mighty hand against the mast.

'Aye!' he growled. 'He was right to shoot it!'

To my surprise, a great murmur of assent went up and down the ship as this theory was finally accepted by one and all. My uncle, who had been standing nearby in the shade of the mainsails, stepped forward warily, blinking into the sunlight.

I could see that he was as surprised as I was when a great gaggle of the crew gathered about him, slapping him and cheering him and wanting to have some contact with him, as though it was he now, and not the albatross, who was the source of good fortune. Such is the fickleness and foolishness of superstition.

Though I shook my head a little with wonder at the about-turn of the crew, still I was glad of it. If the crew felt ashamed of their actions, then I felt more so, for I had a duty of kinship. I joined in the cheers and tried to put the past behind me.

A wide smile appeared on my uncle's face for the first time in an age, and for a while it seemed almost as if the clock had been turned back and we were all as we were at the beginning of the voyage.

It was a dream of course. Nothing was the same. Nothing would ever be the same again.

XIX

So it was that my uncle found himself actually welcomed by the crew. It was astonishing to see. Each day brought hearty claps on his back from young and old, and, though confused at first, when he learned their meaning, he was happy to agree that his actions had been the saving of the ship.

My uncle might not have been telling his stories any more, but he was only too happy to be the hero of this one, however unlikely a hero he might be.

I still felt the shame of having not cried out to stop his hanging and, though he said nothing, I was sure he must hate me for it.

He gave no sign of any bitterness, however. He had recovered some of his old good cheer and swagger, but I didn't altogether believe in it, any more than I believed that his killing of the bird had been the saving of the ship. Or that, even if it had, that had been his intention when he pulled the trigger.

But this made me feel guilty too. Was I being unfair? Maybe my uncle had genuinely felt the bird to be an evil presence. Maybe he really was a hero and I was refusing to give him credit.

The good wind blew and we sailed on, confident that we would eventually make landfall and have a chance to pick up some provisions of fresh food and water. All would be well. We had been plucked from the mouth of hell and I suddenly had an overwhelming urge to make my peace with my uncle.

I went down into the far reaches of the hold where I knew he often took himself when not at work. It seemed the approval of the crew didn't mean he wanted to spend any more time than necessary in their company.

The hold was so dark after the brightness of the daylight above that it was like blindness to step into its gloom. I cursed loudly as I cracked my shin against some unseen obstacle as I fumbled my way, searching for him in the darkness.

I finally glimpsed his pale face through the murk. I had intended to apologise for not speaking up for him when he was attacked. But down there, in the dark, I felt too afraid of him, too afraid to remind him of my treachery.

'Uncle,' I said eventually, 'how can you stand being in such darkness? I can't see a thing.'

'There is nothing to see,' he said.

There was no comfort in his voice. I felt like I was in a cave with a wounded wolf.

'But it stinks down here,' I said.

'Does it?' he answered wearily.

'Yes,' I said. 'It really does. Why do you spend so much time down here on your own?'

He did not reply.

'You see,' I said cheerfully. 'All is well again. You had no need to despair. Perhaps your repentance was heard.'

'Repentance?' he said, with a flash of his old haughtiness in his voice. It troubled me to hear it and I struggled to keep the annoyance I felt from showing in my voice.

'You were sorry for it and now all is well,' I persisted, in the hope he would change his tone.

'No,' he said, shaking his head and carrying on tying off a rope. 'You've heard the crew. I was right all along. I was *right*!'

Even as I spoke, I felt I should simply agree with him and leave. Every second in that place was revolting to me. But I could not bear his triumphant tone.

'Is that why you killed the bird, then?' I said. 'To free the ship and save the crew?'

'What difference does it make why I shot it?' he said, his eyes glowing in the darkness. 'Are we not back on course? Are we not free of the ice and safely through the mist? I saved us by killing that bird. Spare me your grief for that creature. It is shared by no one on this ship.'

I had perceived the same madness in him that day – in the moments before he shot the albatross. He had not changed. It was only the crew who had changed their opinion of him. And it was not to last.

XX

My uncle smiled and talked to the crew when he was working; most other times he took himself off into his little lair below deck. He did not eat with us, nor sleep with us.

This didn't seem to bother anyone but me, and after a while it didn't bother me either. I had nothing to say to him and I felt that only I saw his true nature. I remembered the pilot's son and felt a little like him now, in that I too sensed evil hovering around my uncle.

What could I do? My uncle was right: the whole crew, and the captain too, they all wanted to believe that he had saved them by killing that bird. They all wanted to believe that misfortune was behind them.

And the truth was I wanted to believe it as well. I wanted to be part of this new happier mood. I wanted to believe that everything would be well. Because, as soon as I stopped to think, there was still much to be concerned about.

We were sure of little about our position other than that we were somehow now in the Pacific – waters unknown to most of the crew. The compass had not worked since we had entered the icy seas of the frozen south and we had not been able to use the stars because the mist had obscured our view.

We knew also that we were heading north and, judging by the position of the sun in the now clear skies, we were about to cross the Line – the equator – where the sun at midday would stand directly overhead.

The captain and helmsman consulted maps, trying to decode where we might be, but, until we sighted some land or another ship, we could not be certain. And all we could hope for was that the ship we saw would be a friendly one, or the land we came upon would not wreck us or be inhabited by cannibals or some such.

Day by day, this new uncertainty chipped away at the relief we had felt to be free of the mist. With heavy hearts we all came to realise that we were not free of the enchantment; we had just exchanged one kind for another.

Being able to see for miles was no help in finding our way. All we could see was miles and miles of empty ocean. We were as lost as we ever had been, and now it felt as though we were being teased and toyed with, our hopes raised only to be cruelly hacked down.

And the more we realised this, the more unbearable the heat became. We were in a desert: a desert of salt water. We had seen nothing but water for weeks now. The albatross had been the only sign of life outside the ship. On the entire voyage since leaving Cape Verde, we had seen not even a single fish – no, nor even one strand of weed. And there was no more life in this sun-drenched ocean than there had been in the frozen one.

We had enjoyed the sun after so many days of mist and cold and damp, but we had yet to feel its full force. Now the sun rose to its full height and there was nowhere to escape its roasting glow.

The boards of the ship began to shrink as all the moisture was driven from them by the force of the sun. Flesh was baked along with wood and canvas and all effort seemed too much to bear.

We did what needed to be done at night, the darkness having returned as we had sailed to more northerly climes. Repairs were needed: the shrinking boards were in danger of sending us to the bottom of the ocean as leak after leak was found and sealed.

We sweated the day away, and our sweat turned to steam before it hit the deck. The captain rationed the water we had taken aboard but our need was too great and it was quickly disappearing. The cold had preserved our foodstuffs, but all that we had left now began to rot and fester. The holds were a stinking, evil place.

And so, bit by bit, all the joy we had felt in leaving the grip of the ice evaporated in the heat. As changeable as the sea, the crew began to think again about my uncle and his part in our supposed salvation.

'I told you we spoke too soon,' said the very same sailor who had spoken in my uncle's defence only days before.

'Aye,' said another. 'He might have freed us from the mist, but we were only swapping one hell for another.'

'Who knows if we'll ever sight land?' said the first. 'How much longer can we last in this heat?'

The sailors hushed their voices as the captain approached and went back to their tasks. The captain watched them leave and stepped up beside me.

'What were they saying?' he asked, still looking in their direction.

'Nothing,' I said.

The captain turned to me and his expression made it clear that this wasn't going to be enough to end the conversation.

'They are worried, Captain,' I said. 'We are worried.'

He nodded, looking away.

'They have been at sea too long,' he said. 'The salt gets into your brain.'

'Do you know where we are, Captain?' I asked.

He looked up, squinting into the sun.

'We are very close to the Line,' he said. 'But where along the Line – well, your guess is as good as mine.'

He looked at me and smiled. It was a kind smile.

'No ocean lasts for ever, boy,' he said. And then, after a pause, he patted me on the shoulder. 'Nothing lasts for ever.'

I'm not sure whether this was meant to comfort me or make me accept whatever fate was about to deliver.

The searing temperature heated up the blood of the crew as well. Tempers shortened and fights flared up over trivial things. More than once the captain had to threaten a flogging before the men would calm themselves and go about their work.

My uncle found himself shunned once more and I didn't feel the need to seek him out. Why should I suffer because of what he was and what he'd done?

There was an edge now, a tension all through the ship. It was better not to make eye contact for fear that it might be misunderstood. I'd feared that kinship to him would damn me as well in the eyes of the crew. But I think they had long ago forgotten there had ever been a link between us.

Even when the crew had welcomed him back, he had not taken to sleeping with us. He had kept himself to his favoured dank, dark part of the hold and stayed there whenever he was not called upon to work.

The crew accepted this behaviour and didn't bother him. My uncle could do as he pleased. It was not as though they had ever really come to like him any better than they had before. But it was different for me.

I could not so easily forget him, however much I would have liked to. I was his nephew. Although I could not think of him without thinking of the albatross he had shot without cause or thought, he was still my father's brother.

'Maybe you can look out for him,' my mother had said. I heard her voice clearly in my head. I had thought it a joke at the time. Now it felt like a request I was honour-bound to obey. It made me angry that I could not set it aside.

Eventually, once again, cursing as I went, I was moved to go and speak to him. It wasn't just that he was my uncle, I wanted some sense that he understood what he'd done.

I climbed the ladder down into the darkness. The stink was even worse than before. As usual, he was sitting alone in the hold, lit only by a thin ray of milky light seeping through the timbers above his head.

'Uncle,' I said curtly, more than once before he turned his face to look at me.

He looked at me for some little while, his eyes shadowed and impossible to see.

'What is it?' he said.

His voice seemed to be laced with the humid dampness of the hold. His tone infuriated me again.

'I have come to see you,' I said, finding that now I was here I could not actually think of anything I wanted to say to him.

He nodded and looked away. As my eyes grew accustomed to the dark, I noticed that he had the body of the albatross beside him. He saw my eyes moving towards it and placed a hand on it defensively. The smell drifted towards my nostrils. It turned my stomach.

I had wondered where the dead bird had gone, but had assumed the captain had tossed it overboard. It was all I could do to stop myself screaming at him in fury.

'Why have you got that?' I hissed.

'Why shouldn't I have it?' said my uncle. 'It's mine.'

I covered my nose and mouth and peered forward. The albatross glowed slightly – a dull rotten glow – and I could see that it was decaying, with feathers lost and matted and the flesh revealed was speckled with mould. The albatross's beak was open and its rancid tongue lolled out. Its eyes were clouded.

'Throw it away,' I said, disgusted. 'If they find you with it, they'll –'

'Don't try to take it from me,' he said, fingering the cross round his neck.

The tone of threat in his voice was clear. I remembered that time in the barn, his knife at my throat.

'Why did you do it?' I said after a pause. 'Why did you kill the albatross?'

My uncle closed his eyes and sighed, as though the question bored him.

'You would not believe my prowess with the crossbow,' he said. 'You thought me a liar.'

'You could have shot anything!' I said, angry that he seemed to be trying to involve me in the blame.

'I don't know,' he said, in a quiet voice I would not have recognised as his own. 'I only knew that I must. It felt right.'

'Right?' I said. 'How could it be right? The bird had done nothing to you.'

He turned to me, his eyes twinkling darkly.

'If I had shot a woodcock or a pigeon, you would not ask me why.'

'But you did not kill it for food,' I said. 'You killed it for . . . I don't know what.'

'And what of that nightingale you shot?' he said. 'What was your reason?'

'I never meant to kill it!' I shouted.

'Truly?' he said, with a cruel twist of his lips.

I stared angrily at him and yet he had touched a nerve somewhere. I found I couldn't reply. My uncle dropped his head and his face was swallowed by the darkness. I wanted to strike him but I feared him more than my anger would allow. I turned and climbed the ladder. When I looked his way, there was nothing but blackness.

XXI

I knew then that I had been right. His madness had never left him. It had simply been hidden by the goodwill of the ship on escaping the mist. As I looked back, I saw that all that time my uncle had still stood among the shadows in the grip of . . . I could not say what.

I hated him at that moment. I had followed my father to sea – my father who I could scarcely even remember – and I had been lured here to this hell by my uncle, who I hardly knew.

I must have been mad myself. Better by far to have stayed with my mother who I loved like life itself. Never again! I vowed that if I ever held my mother again I'd never leave her. Not for all the treasures in the world.

My home never seemed so dear when set against this nothingness. I longed to see familiar faces and feel the sweet unmoving earth beneath my feet. I would roll in the grass like a lamb. I was full of such dreams.

Then the wind stopped. Winds come and go, all sailors know that, but no wind ever dropped like that one did. One minute the sails were full to bursting, the next they sagged against the mast and the once taut rigging drooped.

The sea, which a moment before had been furrowed by a thousand troughs and foaming crests, was now as flat as a painted dish. The ship slowly came to a halt and sat as still as if we were back in the ice sheet.

The sun blazed. The sky, the sea – everything seemed to take on its golden colour. It was as though the ship were sitting in a pool of molten metal and we were all melting in one gigantic furnace.

Just as we had been trapped by ice, now we were trapped by a flat and windless ocean. And just as we had been crushed by ice, now we were crushed by the heat.

The sun was high above us now, right over our heads. I stood on the whole of my own shadow and we were once again in a world of silence.

No one dared to speak, to mark himself out for special attention. No one moved. It was as though the whole world had ground to a halt and we had become pictures in some book.

I felt I could not even move my eyes. That motion seemed too big a thing in that still world. I thought I would hear the very movement of my eyeballs in their bony sockets.

It was the captain who spoke first and his voice sounded like a bellow in that silence, crashing through it like a stone through a glass pane.

'Come now,' he said. 'The wind has dropped is all. We've been through worse and lived to tell the tale. Go about your work and that breeze will blow again, be sure of that.'

There was little to do. Because the ship was becalmed we had no sailing work and this was at least a blessing because we could not have toiled in that heat. Yet the idleness was terrible too. We clustered in the shadows and moved as little as we could that day.

In those few hours, with the lack of distraction, the crew once again turned its angry gaze towards my uncle. He had become linked now with any change in the fortunes of the ship. And though we tried to see this becalming as a natural obstacle to our voyage, we none of us, in truth, believed it to be natural.

My uncle didn't care, of course. He had no need of us. It was clear from his face that he thought all the crew were fools and that he should pay no heed to them. He obeyed the captain's orders, but with the air of someone who was pretending obedience.

I wish I could say that I was any different and yet I too felt sure that my uncle's actions were at the core of our misfortune. In fact, I had even more reason to think this because I knew that my uncle's mind was more troubled even than the crew might guess.

They had not heard him talk as I had. They had not yet discovered that my uncle was harbouring the rotting body of the albatross. And as much as I despised him, I wouldn't have sunk so low as to tell them.

I stood at the prow, gazing at the sea as the sun dropped into the horizon, seeming to melt into it like wax. In these waters there was no evening. Night came down like a curtain with fearful suddenness, and with it at last came respite from the sun's heat.

A group was gathered at the side of the ship and the sounds they made brought all of us over to see what they might be looking at.

I squirmed my way to the rail and looked over.

At first I saw nothing other than the night and the still blacker sea marking the horizon. Then I saw that everyone was looking down and I did likewise.

The water was glowing with a dull green light and, under the surface, was a great slimy mass that I thought was weed of some kind. I'd heard of these huge floating islands of seaweed from sailors back at home and assumed that we had been caught in one.

Then I saw the movement: a coiling slippery movement. Strange creatures were sliding over one another, and each new movement sent a shiver through the entire horde and the glow increased in intensity.

The green mass rose up and seemed to reach out slimy tentacles to touch the hull of the ship. The creatures climbed up and slithered along the surface before slipping back under.

All about us was the smell of decay, as though the ship was rotting all at once, whilst the glow was now so bright it illuminated the whole ship and crew with its ghastly light. Blackness surrounded us on all sides, but we shone candle-bright.

Little flares of green and blue and white played across the surface of the water and gave us too clear a view of the hellish creatures there. No nightmare could have been as terrible to see and yet none of us seemed able to turn our backs on this horrible sight.

The vision began to change and the creatures seemed to struggle to escape and the slime became thick and black and smelled of pitch and I could see seabirds raise their heads in silent screams and try to tug their wings free of the morass. Dolphins, turtles, fish of every kind rose out of the slime and slithered and flapped in their death throes.

'That curse has followed us here!' said the man standing next to me. 'It never was lifted! I told you so!'

'Aye,' said another. 'Whatever spirit held us in the ice floe has hunted us down. You can't escape such things. We're marked men.'

There was a great deal of murmuring in agreement.

'Our lives were forfeit as soon as he killed that albatross.'

At the word 'he', all faces looked for my uncle, but he was not on deck. A group of men set off to find him and I wondered if we would see a repeat of the execution the captain had abandoned.

The men returned with my uncle. He had clearly been struck and more than once. He was shoved forward. Then the albatross was thrown on to the deck beside him.

'He's been keeping that in the hold,' said the man who had thrown it down.

There were mutters of disgust and shakings of heads and many more simply looked at my uncle in shock and revulsion. The albatross was well beyond the state I'd found it in last time. The flesh was eaten away and hanging in blackened tatters from bones and cartilage. One wing fell open and revealed great holes where the flesh had collapsed.

I saw men with tears in their eyes and there were tears in mine too. To see a bird that had been so majestic and beautiful reduced to such a state as this was heartbreaking. It was as though my uncle had killed it all over again.

This time though, the crew seemed to have no stomach for a hanging. The mood was more of disgust than anger. The captain stepped forward. Two men were holding my uncle by the arms. He roughly tore the cross from my uncle's neck and hurled it into the sea.

'You have no right to wear that,' he said. 'Stealing from churches. Killing for your own amusement. Sheldon – fetch me a rope. Thin and short.'

Sheldon cut a length of rope and brought it over. The captain tied it round the neck of the albatross and made a loop of it. Then he moved to put it round my uncle's neck.

'We don't all have your taste for killing. We'll keep our souls free of that taint, for now. You can keep the bird, you murdering madman,' he said. 'You shall wear it every day as a reminder.'

My uncle made to protest, but the captain took out his knife and waved the blade in front of my uncle's face.

'You either wear it,' he said, 'or you wear an anchor and we drop you over the side. If you so much as try to take it off, that's what will happen. You will –'

But the captain's voice dried up. When he tried to speak again, nothing would come out. A man nearby called out angrily – or that was his intent, for, just as with the captain, no sound emerged.

One by one each of us tried to speak and each with the same result. We had all – every man jack of us – been struck dumb. And when the silent commotion had settled, those dumbstruck faces turned as one to stare resentfully at my uncle.

The captain dealt my uncle a fierce blow with the back of his hand, and with that the rotting carcass of the once magnificent albatross was hung around his neck.

PART THE THIRD

XXII

The prospect of slowly freezing to death back at the ice floes no longer seemed such a sorry fate, those who had died there simply slipping into sleep never to awake.

We who had survived now found ourselves punished for our survival. We staggered on from one beating to another. And the sense that my uncle was somehow at the root of everything that was happening appeared to be a truth that could not be denied.

Worse than that, he seemed to be protected by the forces that toyed with us. When he was about to be hanged, the ice melted. The captain's voice was taken from him as he berated my uncle, and our voices too.

The crew had gone from disliking my uncle, to despising him to hating him, and now – now they feared him. Had they not, someone would have put a knife in his back and dumped him overboard without another thought.

Instead, my uncle haunted the ship like a ghost, relieved of any duties and skulking among the shadows with the stinking, rotting albatross glowing palely round his neck, its tattered wings outstretched, their matted tips stroking the deck.

This was a horror to match the frozen world. The becalmed and empty sea was already unnaturally silent, save for the slippery sounds of the creatures trapped in the ooze that covered the ocean floor thereabouts.

Aboard the ship, the only din came from the footfalls of our crew or the slight squeak in the hemp ropes as the heat caused some change in tension in the rigging. If someone dropped a tool or knocked over a bucket, it sounded like the gates of hell had been burst open and we had to cover our ears to shut out the noise. And we looked liked the damned too, our poor bodies starved and wasted.

What next? What new sport was to be had with us? I began to wonder if we had already died back at the ice fields. Perhaps we were going from one circle of hell to another and this would go on for all eternity.

I leaned against the bulwarks looking out to

sea and barely had the strength to keep from falling down. My forehead sank lower and lower until it rested on the bleached and weathered wood.

A single bead of sweat fell from my face and struck the deck. It was as though time had slowed and I saw its shimmering sphere plummet and hit the weathered plank, the stain it made drying in a blinked eye.

With no water, no wind, no land in sight, things were hopeless. We did not even have the voice to offer comfort or shout curses or pray for release. The horizon shimmered like the haze over smouldering embers.

I stared at the sea below – at the sticky writhing mass. New creatures became caught up in the dance of death, joining with the decomposing bodies of those already trapped, whilst beneath them I could see plumes of black slime rising from the ocean bed.

I looked to my right and saw my uncle nearby and tears filled my eyes. His head was bowed over the lolling head of the bird, and he muttered noiselessly to himself. He drummed his fingers on the wood of the bulwark and in that silence, of course, it sounded like a rumbling cart.

I wished once more with all my heart that I had

never set foot aboard this ship and never laid eyes on my uncle. I wanted to be home with my mother and would have gladly done the dullest chores and never, never would I have wished for adventure again.

I looked out to sea once more. The sun was setting in the west: a great blood-soaked disc sinking. As the edge met the flat horizon, I saw something appear against its crimson glow, like a speck of dirt.

It was hard to look at it at first. Though the power of the sun was waning, it still burned my sight and I just assumed that it was a trick of my weary eyes and fevered brain. I even wiped my eyes and looked again, thinking the speck might have been in my eye rather than on the sea, and yet it did not disappear but became more solid as it increased in size.

I looked for someone to share this with but the only person was my uncle, who shuffled over, the fetid scent of the rotting albatross coming with him. I flinched at the smell and my stomach clenched.

He saw it too. His head jutted forward like a dog watching a rabbit, his eyes sparkling red in reflection of the sun. The skull-head of the albatross lolled horribly. And then, to my horror, my uncle lifted his arm and sank his teeth into his own flesh, as though he was biting at a hunk of beef.

He bared his gums and forced the teeth down through the skin and into the muscle. Blood welled up around his teeth and lips and he lifted his head, lapping at the blood and licking it, savouring it. It was as shocking a sight as I had seen on that terrible journey.

And yet there was some method in his madness. As the blood moistened his tongue and cracked and blackened lips, a faint sound emerged from his throat. He took a deep breath and opened his mouth, his teeth coated in blood, and the voice that erupted shook the air.

'A sail!' he gurgled. 'A sail!'

The whole crew started with shock at the sound of a human voice and all heads turned to where my uncle stood.

'A sail!' he cried again, louder and more hoarsely this time, pointing to the horizon.

The crew might have been fit and well, so quickly they leapt to their feet and dashed to our side. They saw that speck, that shape, as we did – and saw clearly now, as we did, that it was a ship.

The crew opened their mouths and again no

sound emerged save a dusty hiss. We clambered up the rigging and waved, but these efforts were soon given up as there was no doubt that the ship was already making for ours. And at great speed.

'You see!' said my uncle in triumph, his gurgling voice coated in the blood from his arm. 'She tacks no more! She is headed straight for us!'

His face was wild with excitement, as though he could redeem himself by summoning up this rescue. He leapt about, making the albatross flap and jig like some vile puppet. He grinned a slippery, bloodstained grin.

And it ought to have been a cause for celebration. A ship. It should have raised our spirits. But I saw the face of each man around us fall into first a look of disbelief and confusion, and then, increasingly, a look of dismal dread.

Within moments my face wore the same grim expression, for the sea was as calm as it had always been and not a breath of wind blew. And yet that ship was now close enough to give some view of its details. How could it move so swiftly?

It veered a little in its course and moved between us and the sinking sun. The effect was hideous. The ship was riddled with holes and eaten through with rot and worms. The red sunlight shone between its open boards and black spars like a fire in a brazier.

It sped towards us noiselessly, even though its thin and ragged sails hung limp from broken masts. As it neared us, its rotten hulk became illuminated by the green glow of the creatures that still squirmed about our vessel.

Night fell. The sky turned green then blue then deepest indigo and all within seconds. The blackness of the approaching ship now fitted its surroundings and it looked whole and true again. But we dreaded it.

Was this the Black Ship I had heard so much about? The fabled ship crewed by drowned sailors? I could tell I was not the only one to have such thoughts and men about me crossed themselves and made silent prayer.

It pulled alongside. A ghastly limelight now lit up the wreck and showed the ... I was going to say 'crew', yet that word could not rightly be used for what we saw.

The sight of a crew made up of the drowned would have been a horror, of course, but that ship – the Black Ship – only sought out their own kind as crewmates, and we had not drowned.

There were only two figures visible on the ship and neither of them had ever been a sailor. This craft was wondrous strange, yet these two hellish characters made it appear the most ordinary sight in the world.

My lifeblood seemed to congeal in my veins. My mind was already at breaking point, unable to cope with the horrors that each new moment presented to it. Would this be one step too far? I hoped it would. I hoped my mind would snap and I'd no longer know truth from lie – that I'd fall into some happy state of oblivion, like that of the pilot's son.

Crouched at the prow of the ship, was a woman dressed in a filthy shift that had once perhaps been fine but was now ragged and damp, green with mould in places, and clung to her pallid skin here and there.

And her skin was so white. No – not white exactly, more that queasy pale yellow and blue-white of fat on the meat hanging from the butcher's hook. The lifeless pallor was made even more striking by the glistening redness of her ruby lips and the golden tresses that tumbled around her face.

Her eyes were large and limpid, like those of a fish brought up from the far dark and dismal ocean depths. They glinted and flickered left and right and the ghostly green light with them. They were like those of an animal that has known only night and spent each daylight hour hidden and cloaked in shadow.

She looked more than a little crazed. Her red lips shone like beads of blood on a pinprick and parted to show small, perfect teeth. The tip of her tongue appeared between them as she clapped her thin white hands rapidly together.

She was so strange a creature that she had entirely distracted my attention from the figure who sat beside her. But now he leaned forward, holding a cup, and as he did so, every one of us aboard our ship instinctively backed away to the same degree. This man – no, I cannot say 'man' – this thing in human form was male, it's true, but like some reanimated corpse.

His face was more skull than anything else: what skin was left was stretched tightly like old leather, its taut surface frayed and holed in places, revealing darkened bone and gristle.

If he had eyes, I could not see them, and I was glad of it. He wore a hooded cloak that added further shadow to the night's darkness and made it difficult to see any features other than those I have already described and this robe swaddled his body, as ragged as his face, leaving horrible glimpses of mummified flesh and dark, stained bones.

I knew who he was. We all did. King Death had come for us at last, as he must come for all men. Who the woman might be was less clear. She was not Life, that was all too apparent. She was not anything good, I felt sure of that.

Death leaned forward, his tattered robes moving with him. He held a pewter cup in his right hand and the bones of his wrist were hideously exposed as he rattled the contents and poured the dice on the deck.

It was too dark, even with the glowlight, to see the numbers on the dice, but it was apparent from the way he shook his head and sat back heavily that the score was not a good one.

The female creature took the cup from his hands with a weird little yelp and grinned, her teeth showing pale green between the poppy-red lips. She picked up the dice and put them in the cup, giving it a kiss and looking at us with bulging eyes.

She gave the cup a sudden shake and the noise it made was painful to hear in that silence. I felt it in my brain and in my gut, as if my own teeth rattled in my skull. She stretched out her arm, turned her wrist and out tumbled the two bone dice.

She stared at them in wonder, and turned to her mate in triumph, whilst he shook his head again and clenched his bony fists.

'The game is done!' cried the woman. 'I've won! I've won!'

Then she whistled three times, sharp and harsh, into the night of a million stars strewn above our heads. Death sank back, disappointed, into the shadows and the woman turned to us – and with such a horrible expression of victory and possession that I wondered if we would not have been better off had Death won.

The ghastly woman looked straight at my uncle and smiled. It was such a dreadful smile; I wished that I could have died so that I might never have seen it. She walked slowly to the side of her ship and never once took her eyes from my uncle.

Then, with a lizard-like agility, she clambered up the side of our ship and stood upon the deck. Still she stared at my uncle. And we all followed her gaze as she walked towards him.

Everyone understood that he had brought this upon us. This creature clearly knew it and we knew it. Tears welled in my eyes – of shame and anger and a childish desire to wake from this nightmare and find myself in my mother's arms. But I did not wake.

The woman slowly trod the deck, her feet scarcely making a sound, and all was silent in the world. Her movements were so slow and floating that it was as though she were walking beneath the waves and it seemed to take an eternity for her to stand before my uncle.

Then she made a high-pitched trill and lunged forward, kissing him on the lips. He reeled back, as the creature giggled and clapped her hands like a little girl. It was her most horrible performance yet.

I know not why, but as he backed away from her, my uncle cast a swift glance at me – and the woman saw it. With mounting terror I watched her walk towards me, her head cocked to one side, her grinning lips shimmering.

I backed away as far as I could but soon there was nowhere else to go. I would gladly have taken my chances with the slime-things in the sea – anywhere would have been better than to stay with her – but she held me in a fierce grip with her snake-like stare.

She came close – closer than I thought my wits could bear. I saw my fear-filled face reflected in the pools of her huge eyes that shone with an unnatural light.

She did not touch me. She seemed only to study me, as though I was an object of especial fascination to her. But only for a moment. For quite suddenly she clucked her tongue and turned and walked away to climb back into her own craft.

One by one, without a cry or a groan, and with that vile creature smiling on, each of the crew fell down, and I along with them. We fell where we'd stood, thudding to the deck, straddled across each other's sun-burned and wasted bodies.

I fell in such a way that I looked back towards my uncle. He alone of us stood upright, lit from below by the green glow all about the ship. He staggered back until he hit the capstan, staring in disbelief.

Then the souls of each of my fellow mariners began to rise like smoke from the fallen bodies. They rose and began to swirl about my uncle like a tornado and then all at once they hurtled upwards with a great whooshing noise and disappeared into the night sky. Every single soul of the fallen men had left their lifeless bodies.

Every single soul save mine.

PART THE FOURTH

XXIII

That's right. I fell down with all the others. I died along with them. Believe it. Why would I lie? I died. Make no mistake.

I felt the warm life leave me and I felt my heart turn cold at its flight. I dropped down to the deck and seemed to fall through it, through the hold and through the hull, through the cold waters beneath, to a dismal abyss below.

I sank down through this darkness until I eventually settled on the seabed – though I could see through the gloom that it was featureless. There were no stones or rocks or weed or fish. It was more like the floor of some great warehouse.

The only light was a narrow beam that came from high above. It hit the floor some way away from where I stood and I slowly walked towards it.

It seemed to take an age to reach that small patch of bright floor and when I stood beside it I looked up, trying to follow the beam's path, but it disappeared into the murk high above.

Looking up became a dizzying business, because the darkness was so featureless all about that I suddenly had the sensation of looking down and following a light that was shining up from the depths of some deep chasm below.

I looked back at the patch of the ocean floor illuminated by the beam and as I did so I stepped into its light. In that instant, I was sucked upwards at great speed and found myself once more on the deck of the ship.

I was left emptier and darker, like a deserted house. The blood no longer surged in my veins, my lungs no longer filled with air. Only my mind seemed to remain in my control.

My soul did not flee like the others. It stayed within my lifeless body but it was as if it had been bound and gagged and loaded down with heavy weights.

I had never been aware of my soul before. I gave no thought to such things. But now I felt a terrible sorrow for the loss of its freedom and health and a great fear came over me.

My shipmates lay as empty shells – and they were lucky. They were unaware. Their true selves had gone and only the appearance of them remained. But I would see what happened next.

Each of us had fallen with eyes wide open, frozen in the cursed look we had given my uncle as we fell. What a sight that was! He stood there among us, like a murderer, wide-eyed and awestruck, and a hundred pairs of lifeless eyes stared back at him in the gloom.

I was somehow sure that all those eyes were unseeing apart from mine, though they no doubt bored into his soul all the same. My uncle looked at me just once and shook his head. He had no idea that I was looking back – and I could give him no sign that I was.

The moon rose above us and the terrible scene was lit by its pale light. It looked like a massacre had taken place or we were the casualties in some great sea battle, but our deaths would be unnoticed by the world. No poems would mark our falling.

The ship would surely rot away in time and we would all be taken down into the depths of the ocean to be gnawed at by crabs and starfish. Would I be conscious? Would I feel their rasping mouths attack my flesh?

The Death Ship moved slowly off. I saw its ragged sails slip out of view, like the passage of a flock of bats. It made no sound as it left, like a dark cloud passing over the night sky.

King Death sailed away and took his comrade
with him. I could still hear her chirruping trium-
phantly and the sound of it cut into me like
needles.

She sailed away, until the sound of her gloat-
ing mingled with the sound of the sea and she
was finally gone.

But if she had won, then why had we all died?
Was this woman another Death? And why, if dead,
could I still think to ask this question? I felt sure
this strange limbo state was mine alone and sure
too that it had something to do with the special
interest that creature took in me before she left.
She seemed to sense the link to my uncle and so my
soul did not ascend with those of my crewmates.

She must have been some ghastly not-quite-
death – some horrible merging of two states: a
Life-in-Death. Was this to be my new fate? To
live in death but not live? To feel the grip of
Death: to know its grip and yet not have its sweet
release – to feel its hold forever?

My uncle stood, his mouth twitching. He
seemed to be in a daze. He stared after the retreating ship, his face cold and pale in the moonlight.
His mind struggled, like mine did, to cope with
the strangeness of this new world we found
ourselves in.

And then he turned to us, his shipmates. There we lay, dead – all dead – and all our eyes turned as one to look at him. He put his hands to his face and staggered away.

But when he looked away from us, all he could see was the slimy, writhing sea and the horror of that sight meant he walked back to the centre of the deck and, in desperation, closed his eyes.

It did him no good. He could close his eyes but he knew we were still there, each accusing eye glistening in the moon glow. Why, even if he had blinded himself with a red hot poker, the spectacle we made would only have burned itself more deeply into his afflicted mind.

XXIV

For days and days, we lay like that. It was as if the moment that follows death had been endlessly unravelled and spun out into an eternity.

It was the unearthly stillness that followed a hammer striking an anvil. Time seemed to have exhaled its last breath and left us all marooned. Yet time did move on.

The sun came up and the sun set. The days were cloudless and relentless in the dazzling brightness. The nights were star filled and moon washed. Through both my uncle stood on the patch of deck uncluttered by corpses and hung his head.

I would say 'hung his head in shame', but I didn't believe him capable of such an emotion. More likely he hung his head in self-pity. And yet he lived on at our expense. He lived on whilst the corpses of better men lay at his feet.

I thought of all the stories he had told of his

battles and wondered how many, if any, were true. Had he stood at the centre of such a death count before? Or was it all boasting or wild imagining?

I could detect nothing one way or another from his face. His expression gave little away. He seemed to be in a kind of trance.

And I could do nothing but watch him. Can you imagine what that was like? To never sleep nor even rest your eyes or move your head for want of a different view? To be trapped inside your useless body, peeping through your own eyes as if they were spy-holes?

Hour after hour after hour, I lay there, feeling nothing save a growing disgust for my uncle. My mind was all that seemed to move in that stillness, and yet I could not move it beyond the confines of that deathly ship.

I would have gladly gone away in my mind to happier days and happier places, but, with my eyes held open, I was unable to think of anything except the horror of the present.

Hour after hour after hour, yet we – the dead crew – did not rot or reek the way we should have done. Some magic meant that, though we lay all day in the full force of the sun, we did not change.

The sun should have scalded me but my eyes did not boil in their sockets. My skin did not peel and flake. My body did not bloat and split open like ripe fruit. Nor did any of the dead aboard the ship.

Why? What was the purpose in our preservation? I could not help thinking that we all lay in some great pause before the next act would be played out.

But whilst we did not change, my uncle looked day by day more like a walking cadaver, his eyes sunken, his skin cracked and burned. The albatross was mostly skeleton and feathers now, and still it seemed to weigh him down like a millstone.

No anchor could have bent him more. It was as if he had the body of each member of the crew strung around his neck like a garland.

One evening the setting sun painted the sky red and gold and lit up the timbers of the ship, as though all about us was burning. I wished it were true. I wished the whole ship was aflame and us with it if meant an end to this nightmare.

I tried with all my might to take my mind to another place, and ghosts of my mother and my father and my home did come but they were frail and spectral and they faded like morning mist.

This firelight bathed everything in its glow: the weather-beaten ship, the lifeless crew on the deck and my damned and hated uncle with the tattered remnant of the albatross.

Whilst I stared at him, some small leech-like slime creature had escaped from the general mass about the ship and had worked its way up the hull and now flopped on to the deck, where it slid across the boards in a series of disgusting spasms.

It twitched and jerked its way along, leaving a ghostly trail of slime behind it. It disappeared out of my view and only reappeared as it began to creep and slide across my chest and up my neck and over my face, my open eyes!

Oh, the dread and revulsion as it blocked my sight! And then, all of a sudden, it was gone, and light streamed back. I saw the silhouetted shape of my uncle standing over me. He had clearly knocked the thing away.

He looked down at my face and shook his head wearily. Even the horror of that thing sliding over my eyes could not make me grateful to him for removing it. All of it was his fault. All of this was his doing.

He seemed to understand this in spite of my unmoving face and closed his eyes, and leaned back until he faced the sky, and then he let out a great roar and a moan that shook the ship like thunder.

He turned back angrily, his eyes wild and wide, and he lunged forward, his grasping hand blurring as it raced towards my eye. I thought at first he was lunging at me, but I realised he was grabbing the slime-thing.

He held the creature up to his face and snarled at it as it writhed and coiled in his fist, curling its tail around his wrist and forearm.

It was black and featureless, sleek and slippery as an eel, but with the same eerie green glow as the rest of its kind. It raised what must have been its head and seemed to contemplate my uncle – though I saw no sign of any eyes.

My uncle strode to the side of the ship and I could guess his intention. He was going to slam it against the rail, as a fisherman might do with a lively catch, and then toss it into the sea.

He raised his arm high with the creature struggling in his hand, but just as he was about to bring it crashing down he seemed to freeze. Then slowly he lowered his arm.

His breathing calmed and he once again held the creature in front of his face. This time he regarded it less with anger than with sadness.

Slowly, and gently, he released the creature into the sea.

XXV

Hour upon hour passed by as I watched my uncle standing at the bulwarks, looking down at the sea – though how many, I could not say. I am certain that the sun set, and more than once.

I wondered if he would ever move again and it was startling when he suddenly climbed up on to the mainstays – the braces that held the rigging for the mainmast – the albatross dangling from his neck, his body bowed with the weight of it.

I assumed that he was making his peace with God before throwing himself into the water. And then I wondered if perhaps it was just the albatross that was going to end up in the sea. After all, who could force him to wear it now?

But he made no move to take it off. He stood there for a long time, staring at the sea below, his right arm wrapped around one of the thick hemp ropes. I saw his eyes glisten as tears welled there and overflowed the lids, trickling down his bearded face.

I cursed him all over again at the thought of this last selfish act. How dare he think that he should have an end to this misery whilst I had to endure it for who knew how long?

Why should he have control over his fate when I was held in the grip of a madness he had spawned? Was I to lie here for all time, staring out across these bodies at the passing days?

The red light from the setting sun mixed eerily with the green glow flickering below and I imagined the creatures moving around the ship and cursed them too for living on when so many men had died.

How could it be that our lives had been so easily forfeited on the roll of a dice and these slimy, squirming things were allowed to live on? These men had mothers, brothers, sons, wives. Their lives couldn't be compared to these sea slugs – or to the albatross for that matter.

My uncle's lips moved, but at first I could not make out the words. But then his voice grew louder – or my hearing sharper. To my amazement, he was praying. Praying to the very force who had let us all die at the throw of the dice.

He sobbed to himself and asked for forgiveness and suddenly the rope that held the albatross around his neck gave way and snapped, and I heard the splash as it dropped into the water below.

There was a dazzle of green and golden light from the unseen creatures gathered around the ship. The dancing light played across my uncle's tormented face and then there was a change.

Even though I was some way off, my mind seemed to concentrate my vision, as though I looked through an eyeglass, and I could see my uncle's face enlarged and in sharp detail.

The haunted expression he had worn for so long fell away and in its place was a look I would never have expected to see. It was the saintly expression of the most devout and God-fearing monk. It was a look of love.

Yes – love! He could not have looked more fondly at those repulsive creatures had he been looking at his own children. Why did I have to witness this latest bout of madness? I swear that had I been able to move I would have beaten him over the head and thrown him headlong into the sea to join his beloved slime-monsters.

PART THE FIFTH

XXVI

My uncle turned from the sea and slumped to the deck. At first I thought he had finally joined the rest of the crew in death, but, no, he was sleeping.

I thought I could not contain my anger, that it was so strong no spell could hold it. Yet I remained locked in stillness, silently hurling abuse at his sleeping face.

What right had he got to sleep? What right had he got to wear that peaceful look on his face when we lay all about him, dead before our time? And all because of his spite and that accursed crossbow!

I hated him then. I burned with the hating of him. He slept on and I was forced to watch him, my eyes wide open, always, always open. The night seemed to darken by degrees and I felt so alone, so bitterly alone. I cursed him over and over again.

I begged my arms to move, my legs to shift, so that I could at least crawl across the deck and cause him some kind of pain. He could still feel pain, I knew that. Let me hurt him.

But none of my prayers were listened to. None of my begging caused a single change in the fabric of that nightmare. My uncle slept on and I could do nothing.

The first drop of rain hit the deck like a cannon-ball, it was so unexpected. Then another fell, and another. One struck me on the face, though I didn't feel it. One hit my open eye and I suffered no pain. I didn't even blink.

Soon the sound of the rain was deafening as it raked across the deck and the dead, drumming the faces of the crew and my sleeping uncle alike. I heard it passing through the air like arrows. I heard each drop as it splashed against canvas, wood, rope and flesh.

The night was filled to bursting with the sound of it. Water flowed over the dry decks and dribbled into the hold. It dripped from sodden sails and into empty barrels and buckets, the metallic notes sounding as loud as a peal of cathedral bells.

It flowed over the faces of my dead comrades – it hammered against their open eyes and trickled into their mouths and over their lolling jaws. It soaked their hair. It drenched their clothes until they clung to the unmoving muscles beneath.

I thought my ears would explode with the sound of it and wondered if my eyes could stand the constant onslaught as I stared out, my vision blurred by the pounding rain.

My uncle finally awoke. How he had slept so long was a wonder in itself. He looked about him in amazement, licking the rainwater from his moustache and beard. He picked up a nearby bowl and poured the contents into his mouth, savouring each drop as though it was the finest wine in all the world.

I saw the suspicion on his face at first. Was he dreaming? Was he dead? And then there was a great roaring in the distance. Lightning flashed far off and thunder rolled like drums. A storm was coming and the sails began to shift.

The sailcloth bulged and billowed like the clouds beyond them. The rigging creaked as the ropes took the strain and the deck boards flexed as the ship began to move off.

The strange thing was that the wind from the storm never touched us. Not one single strand of my uncle's hair was moved. What filled those sails I couldn't say, any more than I could tell you what strange spirits now flew through the rigging.

They were like some flying cousins of the luminous things that had surrounded us in the sea. They too glowed, but with a white or golden light, and they flitted here and there among the sails. It was like the stars had dropped and were dancing around the mast tops.

Meanwhile, the storm roared angrily in the distance but still not a breath of breeze moved over us. The rain still fell straight down, soaking everything below.

The black cloud that was above – the source of this deluge – moved to starboard a little and out came the moon again. And then CRACK – down came a bolt of lightning, without a flicker or a fork, straight into the ocean ahead of us.

Again, the lightning came. It lit the scene with a harsh and sudden light, a scene that had looked vile enough in daylight, but which gained a new level of shock when blasted with this merciless light. Again. And again, imprinting itself upon my mind. Each flash worse than the one before, but I could not close my eyes!

Each shock of light was seared into my eyes

and flashed into my mind to live on as a ghostly afterglow when darkness flooded back.

Then there was a groan. And what a groan it was! It came from every body that lay around and all at once, as though there was only one set of lungs and only one throat, and it came from me too.

It came from me too!

It sounded like it rumbled up from the bowels of the earth and the depths of the ocean. Each one of us who had fallen now stirred – as though the power of the lightning had worked some kind of magic on us and urged our dead muscles back to some kind of life.

After all this time, I could move again! Our dull movements were animated in bursts of light that sped them up and made it seem as though the whole ship had come to life to a crazed beat. Each flash showed the scene in flickering motion like the figures in a magic lantern show.

But it was not life. It was a cruel mockery of life. We moved but that was all. The horrible faces of the dead shone out at each new lightning burst and I suffered the pain of knowing that I looked like them. I was their kin. I was undead.

We groaned, we stirred. I had no more will in this than I had before in lying still. The air moved through my lungs and spilled out in sound but it was nothing to do with me. I was just a puppet now – the gruesome plaything of some hidden force. I supposed we all were.

Was this the grim victory of that female Life-in-Death? Is this what had pleased her so? Was it her pale hands that controlled us? Or had she simply left us as bodies without souls, dead but not dead?

And again I knew somehow that even as my comrades moved, they did so unaware entirely. Only me and my uncle had been allowed to think. As the lightning flashed across the faces of the crew, I found myself jealous of them: jealous of their empty heads.

I sensed something had changed in this strange world. Everything my uncle did seemed to have some effect and this new attitude in him – this repentance of his – had also wrought a change.

He was free of the albatross at last. Were we now free of the curse that fell on us when he killed it? Or was this just another act in the same mystery play?

The ship sailed on and, as it moved, we all took up the places we had occupied in life, whilst my uncle shrank back in terror. And who could blame him?

The sight of my old comrades lying dead on the deck was tragic and hard to bear, but this sight was worse – worse by far. This was a scene from a nightmare – a scene from the Last Days when hell bursts like a boil and madness spills out across the world.

The dead moved about the ship like sleepwalkers and me along with them. Their eyes like mine were open wide and stared without a blink or twitch. Each face was lit by the fireflies above and the glow-worms below and at each flash of lightning they burst into blinding clarity. Each staring face was a nightmare from some doom painting. No church wall had such hideous warnings of the rewards of an ill-spent life. No hell could hold more fearful victims.

We each took up our posts. The captain made no sound yet stood as though commanding us and we obeyed his unspoken orders. From a distance, we would have looked a normal, if very efficient, crew. From a distance!

The helmsman strode to the wheel and, lifting both his hands at once, grabbed hold and began to steer the ship. Or at least he gave the appearance of steering, for I was sure he was no more in control of his movements than I was of mine.

Perhaps even more strangely, my uncle – who did have a free will – chose to join us. It was as if he was trying to make the scene less horrible by pretending to be a part of it.

He took his position next to me, not looking at me once, and pulled on the rope as I did. The muscles on his arms stood out as did the sinews on his neck, where our – the dead crew's – movements seemed effortless.

The grim crew scaled the rigging, climbing in silence. Their movements were, if anything, quicker and more agile than they'd been in life. They moved like lizards or spiders. They swarmed over the ship and my uncle clenched his jaw and went about his task, trying hard to blot us out.

Only once did he look at me. He turned his head and stared straight into my eyes, searching them for some sign of recognition. A sign I did not give him. A sign I could not give him. And so he turned away again and never looked back.

We worked as we would have done. We worked hard and the ship sailed on. I did not tire. I felt nothing. One time the hemp rope slipped in my grip and rasped its way across my palm for a minute before I took hold again. I felt no pain. No pain that is except the pain I bore from knowing I was for ever lost.

XXVII

The ship sailed on. The storm still stalked us, growling every now and then, and though we were in the windless eye of it, still the ship sailed on. The sails we worked were full, but full of what? What force filled that canvas and drove the ship? I didn't know then and I still don't.

We worked through that night, sailing on blindly into the darkness. Our limbs didn't tire; our bellies did not growl for feeding. Never could a crew have worked as hard. We'd left the mass of glowing sea monsters far behind and were in open ocean. Then, whatever force compelled the crew to work, now made them stop and gather slowly round the mainmast.

All of us – all of us apart from my uncle, who stood at the stern, watching us in awestruck wonder, trying to decide what new strangeness was about to unfold – clustered together in silence.

Then the crew as one tilted back their heads and opened up their mouths and sang. The sound was like no human being could ever make: more beautiful than the greatest earthly choir. It was the singing voice of angels.

And beautiful though it was, it was yet another torment, because the sound didn't come from me. Of all the undead crew, I was the only one who did not join this heavenly choir, and I knew then that their souls had not returned when they raised themselves up. The emptied shells that were the crew were host to heavenly spirits.

My soul had never left: my soul, with all its flaws, remained inside the husk of body, chained like a prisoner in a cell.

My fate was different to the rest of the crew. Their souls were somewhere else. Who knew where? It wasn't as though they were all good men. Was it heaven that awaited them? I'd have gladly taken my chances wherever it was.

The singing shook the air. The sound of it was like a physical thing. As it left their mouths it seemed to me to take the form of shining angels, and they took flight like a flock of white doves, bright and pure against the sky. They were so beautiful.

The sound-angels flew off towards the rising sun and back again, flitting round our heads, their music echoing round and round, like bird-song and babbling brooks and the sound that ripe barley heads make as they brush against each other in a summer breeze. It was like the music of Nature – of everything that was good in the world.

Just as suddenly, all the crew closed up their mouths and the music stopped. The singing ceased but there was not the same silence as before. The sails breathed and sighed as the ship moved and the water lapped at our hull and again I was taken back to fields of corn and fields of barley and the chatter of water flowing over pebbles.

These noises I must have heard a million times and never thought anything of them, yet I flew back in my mind to my childish self, standing chuckling with delight and clapping my hands excitedly over nothing more than these sounds as I stood on the field's edge with my mother. Oh, to be back there.

The ship sailed on – still without a breath of wind. It needed no further assistance from the crew. We simply stood at our place by the mast and my uncle stood at his place and on we went until the sun was directly overhead.

My uncle sought shade, but the sun beat down relentlessly on me and the other crew, making our damp clothes steam. We should have burned like martyrs on a gridiron, yet still I felt nothing. Nothing. I didn't blink or move a muscle. I was as unfeeling as the nails that fixed the deck on which I stood.

The ship came to a sudden halt as though an anchor had been dropped. It lurched back and then forward again. My uncle was thrown to the deck and we, the undead, managed to shift our stance and stay on our feet somehow. My uncle lay unconscious as the ship stood still on a windless ocean.

I – we – stared down at him from our post. My uncle furrowed his brow but did not open his eyes. We stood over his fallen body in a strange reversal of our previous positions. We stood like a group of murderers over the body of our victim.

PART THE SIXTH

XXVIII

The silence came down again. The only movement was the rise and fall of my uncle's chest as he lay in his faint, and the hairs of his beard trembling as his breath left his lips.

The whole world seemed concentrated on those small movements. Without them, the scene could have been a painting or a sculpture, though one that only a madman would have created.

My uncle lay insensible all that long night, but as dawn's light began to grow and soak the whole place in yellow then it was that I heard voices. Voices. Not sounds of weird music, but actual voices.

Two people were talking. Because I could not move my head I couldn't see where the voices were coming from. Could it be that not all of my shipmates were dead? Maybe they had been hidden away in the hold and escaped whatever foul magic had captured the rest of us?

The voices drew nearer and I realised now that they were dropping down from above. There were no living crew up in the topsails, I knew that: I had seen my undead crewmates swarm all over those masts. Nor did these voices give any sign of movement, as men's voices will when they are climbing whilst talking. Instead they seemed to float down.

And in any case, now they were clear, I knew these voices were not those of any one of us. These were not the harsh notes of fishermen and mariners. These voices had the light sing-song tones of a parson.

'Is this he?' said one of the voices. 'Is this the man?'

I still could not see who – or what – spoke, but I could see very clearly that a light was now hovering over where my uncle was lying asleep on the deck. My uncle stirred and half opened his eyes.

'Yes,' the voice continued. 'It was him. With his cruel bow. It was he who slew the albatross. And the spirit who lives in the land of mist and snow, he loved that bird. And even though the bird did nothing but love these men, still that wretch killed it.'

The other voice was softer and sweeter-toned.

'And he has done penance – and he will do more.'

'How is the ship moving without wind to fill the sails?' asked the first voice.

'The air is cut away in front,' said the other. 'And closes in behind!'

The speed of the ship picked up. I could feel the air rushing past me as we went, faster and faster until the stars above were mere blurs in the heavens. Every timber rattled and quaked as it hurtled through the air, skimming across the wavetops like a swallow across a millpond.

'Fly, brother, fly,' said one of the voices, getting fainter. 'Higher! Higher! The ship will slow and the mariner will wake. We must away.'

The ship did slow and the stars began to settle in the sky once more. The night was still and calm, the moon high and still no breeze moved our craft, yet on it went. My uncle woke and stared around in confusion, wondering what he had seen or heard or dreamt.

His eyes naturally came to rest on us, the undead crew who still stood, lit now by the moon high overhead, and he recoiled with a shudder. We must have been a gruesome sight, gathered there together silently in the moonshadows.

My uncle stared back at us, stared into our lifeless eyes, searching for some sign of fellow feeling but finding none. He seemed unable to take his eyes from ours, almost hypnotised by our gaze. It was clear from the look on his face that he would rather have looked almost anywhere, yet still he could not take his eyes away. Perhaps he feared us more in thought than in view.

But then, with an effort, he closed his eyes and turned his head, and when he opened them once more he was looking at the wide, empty ocean and I saw tears fall down his cheeks. Then he turned his back on us and did not turn round again.

A breeze blew up. But it blew in our faces. It blew across my unblinking eyes as we moved ever on, the sails above us actually filling in the opposite direction to that in which we travelled. But we were a ship of impossibilities. There were no surprises left in the world for me or for my uncle.

Or so we thought.

The first sign of the next wonder was the change that now came over my uncle. He'd been standing in his usual stance: of a man beaten down, his back bowed and bent as though the albatross was still roped around his neck.

He stood that way at the prow of the ship, looking ahead, a silhouetted shape against the cold night sky, like an ink blot on blue velvet.

Then he started to move. He craned his head, leaning forward and peering into the distance. To my surprise, he moved suddenly this way and that in an agitated manner. He gripped the rope that was tethered nearby and slapped his hand on the woodwork to his right. He muttered to himself and this muttering grew and grew until he whooped in excitement.

Then I saw what he saw. A light. A light. The dark shapes on the horizon and a light with it. It was land! It was a shoreline and a harbour and a harbour light!

And as we closed in, the wonder of this sight increased a thousandfold because I saw now, even in silhouette, that this wasn't just any shore. I knew these shapes. Even in darkness, I knew this place. I knew that church tower jutting from the houses on the hill. I'd been christened there. This was my own town: my own sweet town.

My uncle burst into sobbing and I would have done likewise if I'd been able. I heard him mumbling and shaking his head as we rounded the end of the harbour wall and entered its mouth.

It was like a dream. The harbour was deserted.

The only sound was that of the water moving against the side of our ship as we slowed, and then the wake lapping against the harbour wall and rocking the boats moored alongside.

The whole scene was bathed in moonlight. The water was flat calm and mirror smooth and the little cockerel on the church tower glinted and winked its light across the water of the bay and into my own tired eyes as I looked across the scene with a heavy heart and wondering mind. What was to become of us now?

Would my mother come down to the harbour and find me like this? Would the spell now be lifted? Would we now be allowed to die? Would I be released from the spell that held me?

Even as I thought this, I fell to the deck and all the dead crew along with me. We fell with a sickening thud that made my uncle turn with a startled expression.

And over each fallen man stood a glowing figure, hovering like a beacon, lighting the ship like a signal to the shore and illuminating my uncle's awestruck face. The whole scene was lit as though by a thousand candles.

My uncle knelt and prayed whilst away in the distance I heard the sound of oars splashing in the waters of the bay.

It should have been a joyful sound. It should have been a sound of homecoming, a sound of welcome. It should have meant a rescue – a waking from this nightmare. But I knew somehow that the forces that had brought us to this point had not finished with us.

I heard voices. I heard the pilot shouting to the ship and then discussions in his boat between him and others aboard. What was coming next? Were these men about to be swallowed up in the curse along with us?

PART THE SEVENTH

XXIX

I recognised the hermit's voice as well as the pilot's as the boat came nearer to the ship. I heard the hermit wondering aloud why we hadn't answered their call and then marvelling at the state of the sails whilst the pilot moaned and said the whole ship had a 'fiendish look'. He was all for turning back, but the hermit told him to keep rowing.

Then there was a sound I had never heard. It bubbled up from deep below and began to rock the ship. The pilot's boat was almost upon us when the rumble rushed upwards and grabbed the ship and dragged us under.

The sea reared up on every side and then crashed in upon us. The holds filled with water and the crew were sucked down into the watery depths, and the ship sucked down too into the deeps of the bay.

I saw my uncle floating free and heading up towards the moon glow whilst I sank with my crewmates. And I did not fear that fate. I did not fear death. But I did fear this living death. Would I be trapped in that state for ever?

Then I saw that the magic that had held the bodies of my fellows from rotting as they should, now left and each man underwent a month of decomposing in a few short seconds. Their flesh fell from their bones, and the bones crumbled as they were revealed. They were skeletons for only an instant, but all at once they turned to sand and sank in yellow clouds to the seabed.

However, I did not sink as the others sank. I saw the ship melt into the dark below as it was taken under for ever. It seemed to fall to an impossible depth, as though a huge chasm had opened up beneath us and swallowed it up.

Then I was spun round and about with dizzying speed and sent up – up towards the surface like a bubble, bursting into the moonlight.

I had risen some way away from the pilot's boat. I saw the whirlpool left by the ship's sinking. I was far enough to be hidden from their view but close enough to hear what they said.

There was a commotion going on aboard the pilot's boat as the wake from the sinking ship lifted it high up into the night sky, the silhouette blocking out the stars behind.

The men on the boat were babbling in horror at my uncle's appearance. I suppose he must have looked quite frightening to those who had been in this good, sane world all the time we had been in hell.

He had been pulled aboard by the pilot and the hermit and – yes – the pilot's son was there too. The old world I had known poured back in and excitedly I waved my arm and shouted, amazed that I had been given back control of my movements once again.

No one responded to my cries except, I thought, my uncle, who turned briefly, and once only, at the sound before grabbing the oars and rowing for shore as though pursued by sharks. The pilot's son cried out and collapsed into the boat.

'Ha! Ha!' he screamed, clearly remembering my uncle. 'The Devil knows how to row!'

The hermit sat in the prow of the retreating boat and I heard his prayers over the sound of the oars. I watched my uncle's bent back and cursed him again.

'You heard me,' I said to myself. 'You heard me but you left me here to drown.'

Yet I was not drowning. I was not sinking. I floated, though I seemed to have learned the art without any teaching. I simply did not seem able to sink. I was like a cork, bobbing on the surface.

And I could move! After all those days – who could say how long? – when I was a puppet to whatever forces held me, I was now my own self again. Something had changed and I was free. Life had been returned to me.

I called out again to the boat and begged them to respond, to pick me up and carry me to the shore – but no one turned in my direction, not even my uncle. He rowed on and the joy I had felt in my renewed life turned swiftly to anger. I called again. Nothing!

The boat quickly got away from me and I was forced to make after it. I was surprised to find I had the energy to do it after all I had been through. But my arms and legs moved without pain. I did not feel the water, though it must have been freezing cold.

The boat came ashore on the pebble bank between the spurs of the harbour walls. The moonlight rippled on its wake as I swam as quickly as I could in pursuit.

By the time I reached the shallows, the pilot and his son were already staggering away towards the town, the pilot half carrying his son, who was in the grip of some kind of fit of terror.

The hermit was calm though and my uncle sank heavily to his knees.

'Hear my confession, holy man,' said the uncle.

'Speak, brother,' said the hermit nervously. 'What manner of man art thou?'

'I have been to hell and back,' said my uncle. 'I have sailed to the lands of ice and have been pursued by demons. All my fellows were taken. I alone survive to tell the tale.'

'All dead?' he asked.

'Aye,' said my uncle.

The hermit looked out into the bay and then shook his head.

'Then you are blessed, brother,' he said, turning back to my uncle.

'Blessed?' said my uncle quietly. There was something about his tone of voice I did not like.

'For you alone have been chosen to live,' continued the hermit. 'We must celebrate your survival even whilst we mourn their loss.'

I saw a minute change come over my uncle. It was barely visible. It was a slight shift in how he carried his weight, a slight tilt of the head. I had seen it before.

'Perhaps you are right, holy man,' said my uncle, looking back to the spot where the ship had gone down. 'Though I feel so sorry for those poor souls who were not chosen.'

'Aye,' said the hermit. 'That does you credit. But praise be that anyone lived on. You must not blame yourself for their misfortune. These tragic events are beyond our understanding.'

My uncle nodded and hung his head. Yet there was no humility in his posture. The hermit placed a comforting hand on his shoulder and my uncle stood up unsteadily.

'Come, brother,' said the hermit. 'We must find you food and water. You must be exhausted and in need of sustenance.'

They started to walk away.

'No!' I shouted.

Neither the hermit nor the pilot, who was helping his son further along the shore, paid me any heed. But my uncle clearly heard me. He looked round slowly, his face filled with terror.

'That's not what happened!' I said. 'Tell the truth!'

My uncle was gripped by a sudden agony that shook his whole body and he dropped to the ground, twitching. The hermit rushed to his aid and tried to help him.

'My son?' he said. 'What is the matter, my son? All is well now. You are quite safe.'

My uncle tried to stand with the hermit's assistance.

'Tell the truth,' I said again. 'Tell him what really happened.'

Another seizure wracked my uncle and he gnashed his teeth and dug his fingers into his chest and stomach, as though pierced by a dozen arrows.

'What ails you?' cried the hermit as my uncle groaned and howled.

I walked up to the hermit. He didn't seem to see me, though I stood only inches away from him.

'He's not telling the whole story,' I said. 'He needs to tell you the whole story.'

He could not hear me. Only my uncle could hear me and only he could see me. And the seeing and hearing of me was like a rack and thumb-screws to him.

Was this why I had been spared? To force my uncle to tell the truth, for once in his life? Though at that moment I had no idea that his life was to be so miraculously extended.

'I need . . .' gasped my uncle. 'I must . . . tell you how this happened.'

'There's time enough for that, my son,' said the hermit. 'Sleep first and –'

'NOW!' yelled my uncle. 'I must tell you now.'

And my uncle reached out and grabbed the hermit's arm. That was the first time I saw it – the spasm that passes through my uncle's arm and into that of his listener; the first time I had seen the look of hypnotised enchantment that comes over the face of his listener.

The hermit staggered back a step or two and sat down on the edge of a wall that runs beside the beach. The town was silent, as though we were all caught up in our own world and time had come to rest. The only sound was that of the pilot and his son, trudging across the pebble beach, and soon there was no sound at all save for the hermit's expectant breathing and my uncle's voice.

'There was a ship . . .' began my uncle.

XXX

And that was where it began. He told the whole story to the hermit and he became the first of ... well, I cannot even begin to guess how many listeners he has enthralled. I wonder if it will one day become a myth, like the stories of old about the gods and heroes.

From that moment on the beach that night, we have walked the earth together, he growing old and white-browed over the centuries, but I still the boy I was aboard that ship.

We left the town as soon as my uncle had eaten and slept. We left by a route that did not take us past my mother's house. My uncle did not want her to see the man he had become and I could not bear the thought that she would not see or hear me. It was torture enough to be so close to her yet not be able to feel her embrace. Seeing her would only make it worse.

My uncle ages, though not at any human rate,

for the years – the centuries – have gone by and he lives on. I thought that he would fall and die many miles and many years ago, and every day he looks as though this might be the last time he tells the tale. He looks so frail and walks so slowly. Passers-by shake their heads in wonder at the sight of such an ancient out upon the open road. He is taken for a beggar or some mystic, but only those who fate chooses to hear the tale have any inkling as to what he really is.

Just as he was on the ship, he is charmed, and although the cold and frost gnaws his old bones, still he will not die. Is he immortal? I don't know. He is so much weaker now; it seems less likely that he will simply go on and on. And then what of me?

We pass like night, from land to land, with my uncle having some magical gift of language, so that he can tell the tale in the native tongue no matter where we are. Whether the listener is Chinese or African, Spaniard or Turk, it makes no difference. They are able to hear the words in the language they need.

I seem to know the person he must tell and call on him to speak, wracking his body as I did that first time. I get no pleasure from this. Perhaps I did once, but that was long ago. I have no more choice than he. I play my part, that's all.

* * *

My uncle finishes his story and the listener blinks and pulls back from him, staring at the ancient mariner's hollowed face and skeletal body, as though seeing him properly for the first time.

My uncle grabs his wrist and whispers some words and the man nods dreamily before pulling his hand away and staggering back.

'I shall go to church,' says the man. 'I shall pray for you.'

My uncle takes a deep breath and it rattles in his chest like the last breath of a dying man.

'Listen to me,' says my uncle. 'Pray all you like, but know that it means nothing unless you love man and bird and beast. Love all life, however small, however lowly. Do you understand?'

The man nods.

'I think so.'

My uncle peers at him suspiciously and then nods too, seemingly satisfied that the tale has done its work.

'Then go in peace.'

My uncle gets to his feet, painfully and unsteadily, gripping his staff tightly, the veins and sinews standing out on his wasted arms, the rheumatic knuckles bulging. He shuffles away down the lane.

The listener watches him go and stands for a while in a kind of trance before turning himself and setting off in the other direction.

The sun has set and has left a green glow in the western sky. Soon it will be dark and the old man will sleep. Not I though. I have no need of sleep; I am no longer able to be unconscious. I used to long for sleep. Now I can barely remember what it was.

The ancient mariner walks on and I walk with him, though never beside him. He knows I am there, but he never turns round until he hears me call and feels the pain, and his pain is only increased by the sight of me.

I wonder what I look like now. I can see my own hands in front of me and my feet as I walk. I can see that they are pale; they are the hands and feet of the boy I was and am still, though I am a boy with the inner life of a man who has lived hundreds of winters on this earth.

And winter comes again. Even though my feet are bare, I do not feel the ice beginning to form on the moss beneath them as I follow the old man into the oak woods that cover the hillside hereabouts.

I can hear the sea breaking on a pebbled beach

way down the hill. I can smell the salt air and hear the sad cries of roosting seabirds.

The old man's walk is so slow now he is barely moving and the staff he leans against is the only part of him that does not tremble and look fit to break at any moment.

Finally, with a great sigh, he sits down on a moss-covered root and slumps against the gnarled bark of the oak whose leafless branches crane over him, black against the velvet blue of the night sky.

Stars twinkle and, as the old man falls asleep, they are mirrored on the ground as the moon lights up the tiny crystals of frost forming in the leaf litter.

Yes – winter will soon be here, full fanged. The old man can barely move his hands as it is, so accustomed are they to grasping tightly to that staff.

I look down at him and see his faint breathing, the wisps of white breath rising up like tiny ghosts from his thin, cracked lips. His skeletal face, swamped by beard and long matted hair, is scarcely recognisable as that of the man I set out to sea with all those centuries ago.

I walk closer and stand over him, confident he will not wake. The rags he wears soak up the dampness and the cold along with it. The frost performs its silent ministry, unhelped by any wind.

I stare into the woods ahead of me and realise in a moment of revelation that these are the very woods I played in as a boy. That were I to leave the old man and walk on, I would come to my mother's cottage.

But does it even stand there still? My mother's bones will be dust in the churchyard along with everyone I had ever known. Why, the grandchildren of those I knew are long dead.

For the first time since I saw those dreadful creatures on the ship of Death, I feel pain and tears fill my eyes and blur my sight. The pain seems all the more raw for its novelty.

Blurred vision or not, I know this place. Sea, hill and wood. They do not look so very different. But what now? What is this new wonder?

Just ahead of me a patch of woodland is lit from above by an unearthly light and in its centre is the pilot's boy, just as he was when I saw him holding the lifeless nightingale from my bedroom window.

Here again, he holds the broken and bloodied body in both hands. The sadness of its killing comes back to me full force despite all that has gone between. He opens his lips and this time I can hear the words he speaks.

'Let him go,' he says.

And I have a sudden memory – a memory I had forgotten because I must have been so young when it occurred. I had woken with a nightmare when I was little more than a baby and my father had taken me outside in the moonlit orchard and we had heard a nightingale singing.

I had placed my little hand beside my ear so that I might listen more attentively and my father's eyes had swum with tears as he laughed and hugged me tight and held his face to mine.

Tears flow from my own eyes now. I turn to look at my uncle and find that I can hate him no longer. I look back at the pilot's son. I see them – I see all the spirits of the air pressing in on us, forming out of the blackness of the night sky, some fearsome, others beautiful, and even those that are fearsome are beautiful in their fearsomeness.

There are thousands upon thousands upon thousands. The trees shake gently as they pass by, the frost-coated moss shudders as they swim through the air and coil among the roots.

They are whirling and flying round and round, one moment in the ivy below, the next they are playing amid the stars. They are everywhere at once: everywhere and everything.

I look back at my uncle, the ancient mariner, and I see him slipping and dissolving into the woodland floor. His hair entwines about the ivy curling round the roots, and those roots coil in turn about his arms and legs.

Ivy fronds move through his clothes and push through his sagging flesh, dried now and more like the rags that are disappearing into the moss.

His ribs are like the twigs which push between them, his skull, as brittle as a sea urchin, cracks and shatters and collapses along with every part of his desiccated skeleton, so that it is soon hard to see where he had once been sitting. No one passing by could ever know there had been a human being there at all.

And I am glad to see him go. I am glad to see his suffering at an end. And in my gladness I know that I will share his fate and, kept in this unnatural state for an unnatural span of time, we will both, together, fade.

I have no material form to turn to dust, but I know now that I will join those spirits in the air and I am happy to do so. I see the wood below me and the moon shining on the calm sea and the little harbour of my home town; and then I am air, I am breath, I am silence. I am the moment before a dreaming sleeper wakes.

A NOTE FROM THE AUTHOR

Samuel Taylor Coleridge was born in Ottery St Mary in Devon, England, on 21st October 1772. His father was a vicar and Coleridge was the youngest of ten children. His father died when Coleridge was only a boy of nine and he was sent away to Christ's Hospital charity school in London. He went to Cambridge at nineteen but left without gaining a degree. He formed strong relationships with other poets – first Robert Southey in Oxford, with whom he planned to set up a commune in America, and then with William Wordsworth.

He met Wordsworth, and Wordsworth's sister Dorothy, when he moved with his wife Sarah and baby son David to a cottage at Nether Stowey, a village between Bridgwater and Minehead, on the edge of the Quantock Hills in Somerset. They collaborated on a book of poems – *Lyrical Ballads* – published in 1798. This work is often considered to mark the beginning of the English

Romantic movement in literature, and it is here
that *The Rime of the Ancient Mariner* first appears.

> *And till my ghastly tale is told,*
> *This heart within me burns.*

I am fascinated by stories and storytelling, and
much of the work I've written over the last few
years has involved a storyteller, whether it is
Uncle Montague in *Uncle Montague's Tales of
Terror* or Michael in *The Dead of Winter*, recount-
ing his experiences at Hawton Mere. The Ancient
Mariner is doomed to travel the earth, telling his
tale. But what is his tale?

The Rime of the Ancient Mariner tells a particu-
larly strange story. It is a very long poem, full of
incident – most of it very weird and wonderful. I
find it hard to think of the poem without recall-
ing the famous Gustave Doré engravings that
illustrated an 1878 edition. He is only one of
many illustrators to tackle this work, however.
The writer and illustrator Mervyn Peake also
produced some startling illustrations to the
poem – and so have many others.

Coleridge seems to have been inspired by tales
of real voyages and early polar exploration.
Wordsworth said that the poem came about after

a neighbour described a dream to Coleridge which featured a skeletal ship. Coleridge was reading an account of a voyage in which an albatross had been shot at the time, and in conversation with Wordsworth, he began to link the skeletal ship and the killing of the albatross. But that goes only some way to explaining why he might have written it or what the poem means.

It is often described as being a very early piece of work to show a clear ecological message. Coleridge had a heartfelt reverence for life. The Mariner wilfully takes the life of the albatross and there are terrible consequences. But, like a lot of the most memorable stories, it defies such easy explanations. It is first and foremost an amazing feat of imagining. Coleridge himself described it as 'a poem of pure imagination'.

It has influenced many writers. Herman Melville refers to the poem in Chapter 42 of *Moby Dick*: 'Bethink thee of the albatross, whence come those clouds of spiritual wonderment and pale dread, in which that white phantom sails in all imaginations?'

The poem also influenced Edgar Allan Poe's horrific nautical tale, *The Narrative of Arthur Gordon Pym of Nantucket*.

Coleridge inspired younger Romantic poets, although he was to outlive most of them. We know that *The Rime of the Ancient Mariner* was Percy Bysshe Shelley's favourite Coleridge poem and that he read it to his future wife, Mary Wollstonecraft Shelley. It surely must have influenced her in both the polar opening (and ending) to *Frankenstein* and in the undead creature at the heart of her novel, with the poem's terrible Life-in-Death fate for the crew of the Mariner's ship. Mary quoted the poem in Chapter 5:

> *Like one, that on a lonesome road*
> *Doth walk in fear and dread,*
> *And having once turned round walks on,*
> *And turns no more his head;*
> *Because he knows, a frightful fiend*
> *Doth close behind him tread.*

The great ghost story writer M.R. James quotes the same verse in *Casting the Runes* and I also quoted that verse in *Uncle Montague's Tales of Terror*. It precisely sums up the feeling of dread that I aspire to induce in my readers. It is a verse I return to again and again and know by heart, as I'm sure M.R. James and Mary Shelley did.

This Hermit good lives in that wood,
Which slopes down to the sea.

Coleridge was, tragically, a drug addict for much of his life. Opium was freely available in a liquid form called laudanum and it was widely taken as a form of pain relief at that time. The drug can cause hallucinations and Coleridge famously claimed to have written a poem called *Khubla Khan* in 1797, whilst in an opium dream, and to have been interrupted before he could finish by someone – a 'person from Porlock' – knocking at the door.

I stayed in Porlock with my wife one Christmas many years ago. It is on the north Somerset coast. Coleridge, when he wrote *Kubla Khan*, was staying in a farmhouse between Porlock and Lynton, about a quarter of a mile from Culbone Church. We walked through Culbone Woods that winter, as Coleridge, a keen walker, would have done, stopping at the lovely little church there. It was those magical woods by the sea I imagined to be the location of the boy's cottage and of his meeting with the pilot's son.

The nightingales and the boy's recollection of them is inspired by another of Coleridge's poems from the *Lyrical Ballads* – a poem called *The*

Nightingale – in which, at the end, he describes taking his baby son who had woken, crying, out into the orchard plot of their cottage to watch the moon and listen to the nightingales.

The town from which the Mariner and his nephew set sail is not named in the poem, but is generally held to be Watchet. There is a statue of the Ancient Mariner, albatross about his neck, on the quayside there as a tribute to the poem and to Coleridge, the creator of the myth.

> *He holds him with his skinny hand,*
> *'There was a ship,' quoth he.*

I am not exactly sure when Coleridge's *Ancient Mariner* first reached out his skinny hand to grab me. I am certain that I *heard* it first, rather than read it. I would have been eight or nine, I think. I am often asked about the books I read or the books I enjoyed when I was a child, but I almost always forget to mention poems. Poems – narrative poems like this one – have played a huge part in shaping my feelings about what writing is all about. They come from a very ancient place of myths and sagas. Coleridge deliberately set his poem in an unspecified time and used a deliberately old-fashioned language. This has the effect of making the poem sound as though it has existed for longer than it has. It feels as though there has always been a myth about the killing of an albatross.

Songs and rhymes can embed themselves in your soul, whether they are nursery rhymes or pop songs or epic poems like Homer's *The Odyssey*. Anglo-Saxon storytellers would entertain warriors with long poems like *Beowulf* about monsters and treasure and feats of great bravery. We have always loved stories and often, in the distant past, those stories came in the form of poems and songs.

Stories create stories. Here I am, many, many years after first hearing *The Rime of the Ancient Mariner*, writing my response to Coleridge's story. My inspiration for doing so came from one particular verse, as the ship's undead crew begin to move and go about their work on the ship, in grim silence:

> *The body of my brother's son*
> *Stood by me, knee to knee:*
> *The body and I pulled at one rope,*
> *But he said nought to me.*

I wondered to myself, who was this boy, this nephew, dragged, through no fault of his own, into the Mariner's curse? What might his story have been?

And that was where this book began . . .

READ ON FOR A TASTER OF
ANOTHER SPINE-TINGLING TALE
FROM THE MASTER OF THE MACABRE

'Deliciously creepy with lots of twists and turns'
Daily Mail

PROLOGUE

My name is Michael: Michael Vyner. I'm going to tell you something of my life and of the strange events that have brought me to where I now sit, pen in hand, my heartbeat hastening at their recollection.

I hope that in the writing down of these things I will grow to understand my own story a little better and perhaps bring some comforting light to the still-dark, whispering recesses of my memory.

Horrors loom out of those shadows and my mind recoils at their approach. My God, I can still see that face – that terrible face. Those eyes! My hand clenches my pen with such strength I fear it will snap under the strain. It will take every ounce of willpower I possess to tell this tale. But tell it I must.

I had already known much hardship in my early years, but I had never before seen the horrible blackness of a soul purged of all that is good, shaped by resentment and hatred into something utterly vile and loveless. I had never known evil.

The story I am to recount may seem like the product of some fevered imagination, but the truth is the truth and all I can do is set it down as best I can, within the limits of my ability, and ask that you read it with an open mind.

If, after that, you turn away in disbelief, then I can do naught but smile and wish you well – and wish, too, that I could as easily free myself of the terrifying spectres that haunt the events I am about to relate.

So come with me now. We will walk back through time, and as the fog of the passing years rolls away we will find ourselves among the chill and weathered headstones of a large and well-stocked cemetery.

All about us are stone angels, granite obelisks and marble urns. A sleeping stone lion guards the grave of an old soldier, a praying angel that of a beloved child. Everywhere there are the inscriptions of remembrance, of love curdled into grief.

Grand tombs and mausoleums line a curving cobbled roadway, shaded beneath tall cypress trees. A hearse stands nearby, its black-plumed horses growing impatient. It is December and the air is as damp and cold as the graves beneath our feet. The morning mist is yet to clear. Fallen leaves still litter the cobbles.

A blackbird sings gaily, oblivious to the macabre surroundings, the sound ringing round the silent cemetery, sharp and sweet in the misty vagueness. Jackdaws fly overhead and seem to call back in answer. Some way off, a new grave coldly gapes and the tiny group of mourners are walking away, leaving a boy standing alone.

The boy has cried so much over the last few days that he thinks his tears must surely have dried up for ever. Yet, as he stares down at that awful wooden box in its frightful pit, the tears come again.

There are fewer things sadder than a poorly attended funeral. When that funeral is in honour of a dear and beloved mother, then that sadness is all the more sharply felt and bitter-tasting.

As I am certain by now you have guessed, the lonesome boy by that open grave is none other than the narrator of this story.

CHAPTER ONE

I looked into that grave with as much sense of dread and despair as if I had been staring into my own. Everything I loved was in that hateful wooden box below me. I was alone now: utterly alone.

I had never known my father. He was killed when I was but a baby, one of many whose lives were ended fighting for the British Empire in the bitter dust of Afghanistan. I had no extended family. My mother and I had been everything to each other.

But my mother had never been strong, though she had borne her hardships with great courage. She endured her illness with the same fortitude. But courage is not always enough.

These thoughts and many others taunted me beside that grave. I half considered leaping in and joining her. It seemed preferable to the dark and thorny path that lay ahead of me.

As I stood poised at the pit's edge, I heard footsteps behind me and turned to see my mother's lawyer, Mr Bentley, walking towards me accompanied by a tall, smart and expensively-dressed man. I had, of course, noticed him during the funeral and wondered who he might be. His face was long and pale, his nose large but sharply sculpted. It was a face made for the serious and mournful expression it now wore.

'Michael,' said Bentley, 'this is Mr Jerwood.'

'Master Vyner,' said the man, touching the brim of his hat. 'If I might have a quiet word.'

Bentley left us alone, endeavouring to walk backwards and stumbling over a tombstone as he rejoined his wife, who had been standing at a respectful distance. Looking at Jerwood again, I thought I recognised him.

'I'm sorry, sir,' I said, gulping back sobs and hastily brushing the tears from my cheeks. 'But do I know you?'

'We have met, Michael,' he replied, 'but you will undoubtedly have been too young to remember. May I call you Michael?' I made no reply and he smiled a half-smile, taking my silence for assent.

'Excellent. In short, Michael, you do not know me, but I know you very well.'

'Are you a friend of my mother's, sir?' I asked, puzzled at who this stranger could possibly be.

'Alas no,' he said, glancing quickly towards the grave and then back to me. 'Though I did meet your mother on several occasions, I could not say we were friends. In fact, I could not say with all honesty that your mother actually liked me. Rather, I should have to confess – if I were pressed by a judge in a court of law – that your mother actively *dis*liked me. Not that I ever let that in any way influence me in my dealings with her, and I would happily state – before the same hypothetical judge – that I held your late mother in the highest esteem.'

The stranger breathed a long sigh at the end of this speech, as if the effort of it had quite exhausted him.

'But I'm sorry, sir,' I said. 'I still do not understand . . .'

'You do not understand who I am,' he said with a smile, shaking his head. 'What a fool. Forgive me.' He removed the glove from his right hand and extended it towards me with a small bow. 'Tristan Jerwood,' he said, 'of Enderby, Pettigrew and

Jerwood. I represent the interests of Sir Stephen Clarendon.'

I made no reply. I had heard this name before, of course. It was Sir Stephen whom my father had died to save in an act of bravery that drew great praise and even made the newspapers.

But I had never been able to take pride in his sacrifice. I felt angry that my father had thrown his life away to preserve that of a man I did not know. This hostility clearly showed in my face. Mr Jerwood's expression became cooler by several degrees.

'You have heard that name, I suspect?' he asked.

'I have, sir,' I replied. 'I know that he helped us after my father died. With money and so forth. I had thought that Sir Stephen might be here himself.'

Jerwood heard – as I had wanted him to hear – the note of reproach in my voice and pursed his lips, sighing a little and looking once again towards the grave.

'Your mother did not like me, Michael, as I have said,' he explained, without looking back. 'She took Sir Stephen's money and help because she had to, for her sake and for yours, but she only ever took the barest minimum of what was offered. She was a very proud woman, Michael. I always respected that. Your mother resented the money – and her need for it – and resented me for being the intermediary. That is why she insisted on employing her own lawyer.'

Here he glanced across at Mr Bentley, who stood waiting for me by the carriage with his wife. I had been staying with the Bentleys in the days leading up to the funeral. I had met him on many occasions before, though only briefly, but they had been kind and generous. My pain was still so raw, however, that even such a tender touch served only to aggravate it.

'She was a fine woman, Michael, and you are a very lucky lad to have had her as a mother.'

Tears sprang instantly to my eyes.

'I do not feel so very lucky now, sir,' I said.

Jerwood put his hand on my shoulder. 'Now, now,' he said quietly. 'Sir Stephen has been through troubled times himself. I do not think this is the right time to speak of them, but I promise you that had they not been of such an extreme nature, he would have been at your side today.'

A tear rolled down my cheek. I shrugged his hand away.

'I thank you for coming, sir – for coming in his place,' I said coolly. I was in no mood to be comforted by some stranger whom, by his own admission, my mother did not like.

Jerwood gave his gloves a little twist as though he were wringing the neck of an imaginary chicken. Then he sighed and gave his own neck a stretch.

'Michael,' he said, 'it is my duty to inform you of some matters concerning your immediate future.'

I had naturally given this much thought myself, with increasingly depressing results. Who was I now? I was some non-person, detached from all family ties, floating free and friendless.

'Sir Stephen is now your legal guardian,' he said.

'But I thought my mother did not care for Sir Stephen or for you,' I said, taken aback a little. 'Why would she have agreed to such a thing?'

'I need not remind you that you have no one else, Michael,' said Jerwood. 'But let me assure you that your mother was in full agreement. She loved you and she knew that whatever her feelings about the matter, this was the best option.'

I looked away. He was right, of course. What choice did I have?

'You are to move schools,' said Jerwood.

'Move schools?' I said. 'Why?'

'Sir Stephen feels that St Barnabas is not quite suitable for the son – the ward, I should say – of a man such as him.'

'But I am happy where I am,' I said stiffly.

Jerwood's mouth rose almost imperceptibly at the corners.

'That is not what I have read in the letters Sir Stephen has received from the headmaster.'

I blushed a little from both embarrassment and anger at this stranger knowing about my personal affairs.

'This could be a new start for you, Michael.'

'I do not want a new start, sir,' I replied.

Jerwood let out a long breath, which rose as mist in front of his face. He turned and looked away.

'Do not fight this,' said Jerwood, as if to the trees. 'Sir Stephen has your best interests at heart, believe me. In any event, he can tell you so himself.' He turned back to face me. 'You are invited to visit him for Christmas. He is expecting you at Hawton Mere tomorrow evening.'

'Tomorrow evening?' I cried in astonishment.

'Yes,' said Jerwood. 'I shall accompany you myself. We shall catch a train from –'

'I won't go!' I snapped.

Jerwood took a deep breath and nodded at

Bentley, who hurried over, rubbing his hands together and looking anxiously from my face to Jerwood's.

'Is everything settled then?' he asked, his nose having ripened to a tomato red in the meantime. 'All is well?'

Bentley was a small and rather stout gentleman who seemed unwilling to accept how stout he was. His clothes were at least one size too small for him and gave him a rather alarming appearance, as if his buttons might fly off at any moment or he himself explode with a loud pop.

This impression of over-inflation, of over-ripeness, was only exacerbated by his perpetually red and perspiring face. And if all that were not enough, Bentley was prone to the most unnerving twitches – twitches that could vary in intensity from a mere tic or spasm to startling convulsions.

'I have informed Master Vyner of the situation regarding his schooling,' said Jerwood, backing away from Bentley a little. He tipped his hat to each of us. 'I have also informed him of his visit to Sir Stephen. I shall bid you farewell. Until tomorrow, gentlemen.'

I felt a wave of misery wash over me as I stood there with the twitching Bentley. A child's fate is always in the hands of others; a child is always so very powerless. But how I envied those children whose fates were held in the loving grip of their parents and not, like mine, guided by the cold and joyless hands of lawyers.

'But see now,' said Bentley, twitching violently. 'There now. Dear me. All will be well. All will be well, you'll see.'

'But I don't want to go,' I said. 'Please, Mr Bentley, could I not spend Christmas with you?'

Bentley twitched and winced.

'Now see here, Michael,' he said. 'This is very hard. Very hard indeed.'

'Sir?' I said, a little concerned at his distress and what might be causing it.

'I'm afraid that much as Mrs Bentley and I would love to have you come and stay with us, we both feel that it is only right that you should accept Sir Stephen's invitation.'

'I see,' I said. I was embarrassed to find myself on the verge of tears again and I looked away so that Bentley might not see my troubled face.

'Now then,' he said, grabbing my arms with both hands and turning me back to face him. 'He is your guardian, Michael. You are the ward of a very wealthy man and your whole life depends upon him. Would you throw that away for one Christmas?'

'Would he?' I asked. 'Would he disown me because I stay with you and not him?'

'I would hope not,' he said. 'But you never know with the rich. I work with them all the time and, let me tell you, they are a rum lot. And if the rich are strange, then the landed gentry are stranger still. You never know what any of them will do . . .'

Bentley came to a halt here, realising he had strayed from the point.

'Go to Hawton Mere for Christmas,' he said quietly. 'That's my advice. That's free advice from a lawyer, Michael. It is as rare and as lovely as a phoenix.'

'No,' I said, refusing to change my grim mood. 'I will not.'

Bentley looked at the ground, rocked back and forth on his heels once or twice, then exhaled noisily.

'I have something for you, my boy. Your dear mother asked me to give this to you when the time came.'

With those words he pulled an envelope from his inside coat pocket and handed it to me. Without asking what it was, I opened it and read the enclosed letter.

Dear Michael,

You know that I have always hated taking anything from that man whose life your dear father saved so nobly at the expense of his own. But though each time I did receive his help it made me all the more aware of my husband's absence and it pained my heart – still I took it, Michael, because of you.

And now, because of you, I write this letter while I still have strength, because I know how proud you are. Michael, it is my wish – my dying wish – that you graciously accept all that Sir Stephen can offer you. Take his money and his opportunities and make something of yourself. Be everything you can. Do this for me, Michael.

As always and for ever,
Your loving mother

I folded the letter up and Bentley handed me a handkerchief for the tears that now filled my eyes. What argument could I have that could triumph against such a letter? It seemed I had no choice.

Bentley put his arm round me. 'There, there,' he said. 'All will be well, all will be well. Hawton Mere has a moat, they tell me. A moat! You shall be like a knight in a castle, eh? A knight!' And at this, he waved his finger about in flamboyant imitation of a sword. 'A moated manor house, eh? Yes, yes. All will be well.'

I dried my tears and exhaustion came over me. Resistance was futile and I had no energy left to pursue my objection.

'Come, my boy,' said Bentley quietly. 'Let us quit this place. The air of the graveyard is full of evil humours – toxic, you know, very toxic indeed. Why, I knew a man who dropped down dead as he walked away from a funeral – dead before he reached his carriage. Quite, quite dead.'

Bentley ushered me towards his carriage and we climbed inside. The carriage creaked forward, the wheels beginning their rumble. I looked out of the window and saw my mother's grave retreat from view, lost among the numberless throng of tombs and headstones.

MISTER CREECHER

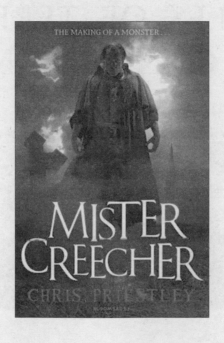

'A brilliant counterpoint to
Frankenstein, compellingly written'
Chris Riddell

'This exciting, affecting and bloody story is a
clever tribute to an enduring classic'
Financial Times

'A beautifully written gothic metafiction'
The Times

THE
TALES OF TERROR
COLLECTION

 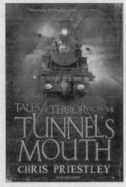 

'Wonderfully macabre and beautifully
crafted horror stories'
Chris Riddell

'Guaranteed to give you nightmares'
Observer

'A delightfully scary book'
Irish Times

THROUGH DEAD EYES

'*Through Dead Eyes* is unbearably gripping'
The Times

'A creepy, tightly plotted psychological thriller . . . chilling'
Telegraph